Good God, What Had He Gotten Himself Into?

"Which way is Miss Benton's classroom?" Mike asked.

"Right this way."

Mike looked at the teacher... and there she was! He was stunned by her, and he wanted to just stare. He stood in the doorway, immobilized.

"Hello. I'm Sara Benton." Sara turned just as he filled the door. He was still dressed in combat fatigues. It looked as though he had just left the battlefield and headed straight for Byford.

He coughed and smiled and walked into the room. He could feel the moisture in his eyes, so he coughed again. He nodded to the prim Sara Benton, then looked at the children, and he knew all of them.

"I'm still a little wobbly. Do you mind if I sit down?"

"Are you all right?"

He turned his head, and gave her an appreciative head-to-toe appraisal.

"I've never felt better in my life!"

Dear Reader,

Welcome to Silhouette Desire! The fabulous things we have to offer you in Silhouette Desire just keep on coming. October is simply chock-full of delicious goodies to keep even the most picky romance reader happy all month long.

First, we have a thrilling new *Man of the Month* book from talented author Paula Detmer Riggs. It's called *A Man of Honor,* and I know Max Kaler is a hero you'll never forget.

Next, Annette Broadrick's SONS OF TEXAS series continues with *Courtship Texas Style!* Please *don't* worry if you didn't catch the beginning of this series, because each of the SONS OF TEXAS stands alone (and how!).

For those of you who are Lass Small fans—and you all know who you are!—her connecting series about those FABULOUS BROWN BROTHERS continues with *Two Halves.* Again, please don't fret if you haven't read about the *other* Brown Brothers, because Mike Brown is a hero in his own right!

I'm always thrilled to be able to introduce new authors to the Silhouette Desire family, and Anne Marie Winston is someone you'll be seeing a lot of in the future. Her first published book ever, *Best Kept Secrets,* is highlighted this month as a PREMIERE title. Watch for future Desire books by this talented newcomer in Spring 1993.

This month is completed in a most delightful way with Jackie Merritt's *Black Creek Ranch* (a new book by Jackie is always a thrill) and Donna Carlisle's *It's Only Make Believe.*

As for November . . . well, I'd tell you all about it, but I've run out of space. You'll just have to wait!

So until next month, happy reading,

Lucia Macro
Senior Editor

LASS
SMALL
TWO HALVES

SILHOUETTE *Desire*

Published by Silhouette Books New York

America's Publisher of Contemporary Romance

SILHOUETTE BOOKS
300 East 42nd St., New York, N.Y. 10017

TWO HALVES

Copyright © 1992 by Lass Small

ISBN: 0-373-05743-1

First Silhouette Books printing October 1992

All the characters in this book have no existence
outside the imagination of the author and have
no relation whatsoever to anyone bearing the same
name or names. They are not even distantly
inspired by any individual known or unknown
to the author, and all incidents are pure invention.

Printed in the U.S.A.

LASS SMALL

finds living on this planet at this time a fascinating experience. People are amazing. She thinks that to be a teller of tales of people, places and things is absolutely marvelous.

My Sources:
Teri Letizia, a superb surgical nurse;
Rick Ritter, who served in Vietnam;
My son-in-law, Roger Johnson, who was once in a
submarine that sat silently on the bottom of the sea;
The local Army recruiting office, which listed all the
gear a man carries into desert.

One

The president called it Desert Storm. It was aptly named. There was sand, no cover, no place to hide. It was another war. Thirty-six-year-old Regular Army M. Sgt. Michael Brown had been in a couple.

Very carefully Mike lay on a cot in a field hospital. They wouldn't let him smoke because he had been hit by shrapnel. Those were shell fragments, which were named for Henry Shrapnel, a British Artillery officer.

Connected to a bag of saline solution, Mike had been evacuated. Oozing blood, he felt like an abused pincushion. He had been deposited in a holding area, and then he was carefully moved to the cot and a plasma sack had been added to his saline needle.

They told him he was okay, but they always said that first. He could see through both eyes and he could swallow. He could wiggle his fingers and toes.

He was aware of the busyness of the area. There were groans from some of the wounded, and one guy was out of his head with delirium. People were hurrying around. There were shouts and calls for specific things.

There was a constant, intent checking of those waiting for care. The medical staff touched the top of Mike's head each time, so that he would know they were there. The top of his head was probably the only place where he was not bleeding.

In a mumble, he asked one, "Did it castrate me?"

And the guy softly laughed in sympathy. "No."

So Mike relaxed.

When the medical team got to Mike, they took out those pieces of shrapnel that were immediately dangerous to his life, but they left the rest alone.

Since the body will slowly reject anything foreign, the pieces of metal would work their way to the skin surface. Or the natural immune mechanism would encapsulate the pieces with scar tissue.

When Mike had been stabilized and could handle the trip, he was flown to Germany. There, he was more carefully examined and the doctors removed more shrapnel pieces that could potentially be life-threatening. But there were still those embedded pieces that would have to be dealt with at another time.

His gear caught up with him. And as he waited in Germany to go home, he reread his mail. He read his adoptive father Salty's one-line communications and smiled. He reread his step mother Felicia's chatty monthly family newsletters, and he read the stack that was addressed: To Any Soldier. After he'd replied during the boredom of waiting for the war to start, the letters were addressed to Mike.

There were a sheaf of them. He'd saved them all. The writing was some better as they went along. Their spelling was inventive. He was impressed that the teacher had resisted correcting the kids' spelling.

He studied the two class pictures, which were labeled with their names. Someone had taken them with a regular camera and the pictures had been enlarged. He'd memorized their names during a waiting time of dead boredom.

The kids were third graders in the town of Byford, Indiana. The teacher wasn't looking at the camera. She was laughing in one and turning to share that with someone off to the side, so she was a little blurred. In the other, she was leaning over to say something to a laughing kid. That was Teddy. He was probably a handful.

Mike felt a sympathy for the kid. He had been one of those kids, always in trouble, when he was that age, but he didn't remember having Teddy's laughter.

Mike would close his eyes and put a ring on the picture, look down and guess the name. He got really good at naming the kids.

Who would have ever believed that Michael Brown of Temple, Ohio, would be sitting in a German hospital glad to have a picture of a third-grade class from Byford, Indiana?

The army life suited Mike Brown. He was not an entirely civilized man. Maybe he just wasn't domesticated. He'd never been tempted to settle down.

He was about five feet ten inches tall and obviously masculine. Men can be male without being that masculine. From being in the Gulf, his hair was sun-streaked and his lashes were white-tipped. His eyes were blue. His lower lip was a little fuller. He didn't smile a lot.

When the time came for him to go back to the States, he still moved cautiously. His skin rips weren't entirely healed, but he could go home.

"How will I get through airport security?" he asked the orderly helping him gather his things.

"You aren't carrying enough."

"How crass of you to say that, when the doctors frown over what's left inside me." A typical statement he could have gleaned from his adoptive mother Felicia who was an actress.

"One man's meat—" The orderly grinned and shrugged.

In disgust, Mike groused, "Good God."

He went back to his base in Texas and was granted convalescent leave. Given copies of his papers, he was told to check in with a CHAMPUS doctor until given a medical clearance to return to duty. CHAMPUS was civilian medical help available to military personnel in this country.

Mike flew home.

Home was Temple, Ohio, which sat south of Cleveland on the southwest turn of the northbound Cuyahoga River.

Mike eased out of the taxi, paid the fare, and the taxi left. Mike stood, looking around. It was spring. March. It was chilly and crisp, the grass was green and the tree leaves were still just hard buds. The walnut trees were bare since the walnuts were always the last to leaf.

The branches of the big elm in the side yard spread out over the area by the porch, and over that space where everybody parked their cars.

Beyond the parking area was the slanting barn and behind that was the tractor shed. Helen the cow was watching him with tolerance as she chewed her cud. And the unridable pony was moving away with some caution. He probably remembered the times Mike had insisted on riding him.

Mike's adoptive father, Salty, came out on the porch and stood watching the second eldest of his assorted children. He was smiling but silent. An ex-navy man, he was almost seventy, but who would ever believe that?

Mike thought Salty looked the same as he had all those years ago when, as a bachelor, Salty had adopted him and John to add to his family who, then, had numbered only a recently adopted Rod. Because Salty had been thirty-six at the time, Mike now felt he still had the time to create his own family, just as Salty had done. But where would he ever find a Felicia? Where would he find a woman who'd taken in so many kids and given him five of his own?

Without words, Mike went slowly up onto the porch and the two men hugged each other without words. As Salty hugged Mike, he was very careful of his shrapnel-filled son.

Felicia came out and flung herself against Mike with the gentle violence of her emotion at seeing him again. Then the three stood there, still silent, very emotional, just looking at each other.

The only obvious change was Mike's very tanned skin, which even the hospital stay hadn't particularly lightened, and there were the healing cuts across his forehead and cheek. His brows were sun-lightened and his blue eyes were tired.

It took days for his parents to let Mike from their sight. If one wasn't with him, the other was. His parents' six youngest adopted kids demanded stories from Mike. "What was it like?" Actually, the intent ones were only the four oldest, who were boys. The little girls, who were both six, were somewhat shy and just watched. One was called Pansy because she had such big eyes.

Mike didn't know them very well. And Teller—Mike didn't know him at all.

There were telephone calls from Mike's distant foster and adopted kin, and there were those who came home to see for themselves that Mike was all right.

But as zapped as he was, Mike did notice things. "I see the house still isn't painted."

"Well, you know Abner fell three years ago."

"I could help."

"It's still too cold." There wasn't any way at all that they'd allow this fragile son to do anything physical.

"You do know that what I do won't make any difference? What will be, will be. I just have to take it a little slow until the original cuts and the incisions heal. And it would be nice if I can forget that I have some stuff floating around loose in my body." He smiled and scratched a match aflame, to light his cigarette.

"I thought you quit." While Salty's rasping voice sounded like a reason not to smoke, his throat had been harmed when he was a young boxer in the navy.

Mike shrugged. "There wasn't much to do over there."

"You'll have to smoke on the porch. And try not to smoke in front of the kids. You make it look macho."

Mike snorted.

"You don't feel macho?"

"I feel like a china plate that's been glued back together by an amateur."

Salty could see that, and he comforted this son. "I remember a time of feeling that way. You'll be okay."

"Did it scare you?"

"We were so busy, and on ship that way, we couldn't get away from it."

Mike added in understanding "—and you were very young."

"It hurts the same, no matter how old you are."

"It's my first experience of feeling that I'm not immortal."

Salty sympathized. "That's always a shock."

And another time, as they lounged before the fireplace and watched the wood crackling, Mike mentioned, "I thought I'd go over and see Rod. There's some third graders in Byford who've been writing to me. Byford's just on past Fort Wayne. I thought I'd go over and see those kids. They wrote me a lot of letters."

Salty encouraged that: "Good idea. Go in full combat dress and let them see you."

Mike looked off to the fields for a time before his glance came back to his father. "I wouldn't want to appear too interesting. War is nasty."

"They deserve to see you like that first. It was an important time for them, and your letters were important in making them feel they knew someone out there."

"Yeah."

After a pause, Salty said quietly, "You know Rod's wife is poorly? She doesn't communicate at all."

"Is that right?" Mike frowned. "She was never one to chatter."

"She doesn't talk at all. Her problems are emotional. She is just different."

"That poor woman."

Salty's voice rasped even more. "My poor son. There is no changing for her. And he won't leave her."

Mike only nodded to indicate he'd heard.

"It'll be good for Rod to see you. I've got a blue car in the back lot that ought to suit you. Try it out."

"My thanks."

So Mike did leave. Wearing soft denims, he got into the confines of the automobile with some care, and he found it a bit surprising that he was comfortable.

It took a while. He drove west to Toledo, down to Fort Wayne, and through that city to Rod's place of business. Rod had a car parts and supply place, where brakes and mufflers were fixed and oil was changed. With their father's car dealership, it wasn't too surprising for a son to be doing something similar.

Additionally, the eldest of Salty and Felicia's actual children, their brother Bob's wife Jo, a teacher, was a part-time mechanic. And Bob's biological brother, Cray, was involved in the same business down in San Antonio. Since none of them was blood kin to Rod, it had to be a skill absorbed by osmosis. Or maybe it was just that Salty saw to it that all his actual and acquired kids learned how to take care of things and to fix them.

In Fort Wayne, Rod was exuberant to see Mike, and looked first to be sure Mike's hand was not injured before he grasped it, but he didn't pound Mike's shoulders and he didn't hug him. He was afraid of hurting him.

But Mike hugged Rod. "I could have used you out there."

"Bad fighting?"

"Long, dark, scary nights, with a lot of scary flickering lights in the sky and sounds that weren't thunder."

Rod replied seriously, "That would tend to make you sort out your brownie points with God."

Mike agreed, "Me and you, Lord."

"Sit down. Coffee?"

"I've had so much coffee in these last nine months that I think I'd like a beer."

"We'll have to leave the premises for that. I don't allow it around."

"Naturally."

"We'll stop on the way to the house. Uh . . . I have to tell you about Cheryl."

"Salty did."

Rod let out his breath. "Good. You needed to be warned."

"I'm sorry."

"Yeah." Rod looked out the door. Then he looked at his brother. "Tell me about you. Are you all right?"

"On the mend."

"Thank God. We all sweat."

Mike gave his head one shake. "I helped."

"Was that whole exercise for the oil? Or was it to test the weapons?"

"You expect a *sergeant* to know that?"

"Why didn't you ever have any ambition for a higher rank?"

"And make wider decisions? Involving more people? I can only take care of just so many people at a time."

Rod grinned. "Yeah. I know. How're the parents?"

"I was looking at them and, you know, they look as they always have. Salty is my inspiration. I figure I'll adopt some kids when I get settled. I'll make a family of my own. He did it. I can, too."

"Yeah. You could." Rod was somber and his eyes were screened by his eyelashes.

"Can you leave now?"

"Sure. Let's go."

"Do you need to call Cheryl?"

"She doesn't answer the phone."

"Oh." Mike didn't really understand, but he needed to indicate that he'd heard.

They spent some time together at an almost empty bar. They talked. Rod was curious and, to him, Mike could talk. It was a release to share the time and to have such a listener, who could take the confidences and understand them. Rod knew Mike. Rod wouldn't suffer echoed anguish over the residue of Mike's past trials or fears. He'd understand.

Mike realized that not many people have such a listener. Too many people have no one with whom they can be completely honest.

When it came time for the evening meal, they went to a Casa d'Angelo's and had superb Italian food. They continued their exchange, and Rod listened.

Mike said with a slight smile, "How did Salty know, just over thirty years ago, that I would need you now to listen to me?"

"Well, he is brilliant with people. But, how did he know how important it would be for me to listen? It's as if I was there with you. You're a good talker. And you're a brave man."

"I'm not so sure."

"A man who does what he has to and gets his own men out of a place like that, has to have a special bravery."

"I was scared spitless."

"But you still did it."

"I was responsible."

"That's the point. Under those circumstances, if you hadn't been scared, you'd'a been stupid."

Mike smiled and made a self-derisive noise through his nose in a puff. He shook his head. "Every man should have a big brother like you." The he asked curiously, "What do you do for a big brother?"

"We have Salty."

"Yeah, but I couldn't talk to Salty."

"But he was there, and you could be around him. He's our anchor."

Mike nodded a little.

"Stay at the house?"

"Tonight. Thanks. I'm going over to Byford. A third-grade class there has been writing to me, and I thought I'd drop in and see them . . . to thank them."

"Call the principal first and clear it."

"I should." Mike agreed to that.

"We'll go on to the house and get you settled. I know you're tired. I can't tell you what it's meant to me to have this visit."

"And for me."

"—but I need to warn you not to expect any reaction at all from Cheryl. She just watches TV and never says a word."

"Has anyone checked her out?"

"They think she ought to be in a home."

"Ahhh."

"I can't allow that."

"God, man. Can't anything be done?"

"No. Medical people visit her. They say she's contented. She doesn't need supervision, just care. She's harmless."

"But—"

"I swore for better or worse."

And it was as Rod had warned. They went into the house and Mike was instantly aware of the smell. There sat the lump that once had been Cheryl. She never took her eyes from the television.

Even so, Mike said, "Hello, Cheryl. It's Mike."

She didn't look up or even blink.

"See?" Rod touched Mike's arm. "Come on. I'll show you where to sleep."

The house was all on one floor. There were three bedrooms and two baths. Rod saw that Mike had what he needed before Mike said, "Good night, Rod. Thanks for listening."

"My pleasure, little brother. I hope you sleep comfortably."

And Mike settled down in the room and slept. He wakened once, very alert. An odd odor was close. Mike didn't move. All his senses were alarmed, but it was different from the war nerves. Slitting his eyes, he looked around without moving a hair.

Cheryl was beside his bed looking at him. Somehow that spooked Mike. He monitored his breathing to be quiet. She just stood there. He didn't know if he should speak or what he should do. He waited what seemed an interminable time, and finally she left silently, walking very slowly. Then with equal slowness, she went through and closed the door soundlessly. Mike was a long time settling down. It was as if he'd been visited by a wraith.

The next day, again wearing the soft denims, Mike put his things back into his car and went down to Rod's place of business with him. He made the call to the principal of the Stephen Decatur Elementary School in Byford. She checked with the third-grade teacher, Miss Benton, before she gave Mike permission to visit the next day.

So Mike had lunch with Rod, and then he left Ford Wayne and drove west to Byford.

Byford was a nice-sized town. The people from the surrounding farms came to Byford, and the community hospital was on the edge of town. Mike drove around the courthouse square. The courthouse was an elaborately fancy building that looked like a castle. And the buildings facing it around the square were like the gentry standing in attendance. One or two of the stores could have been cleaned-up peasants.

It was a tidy town that had been cared for. Most of its money came from the surrounding farms. There was no industry, no smokestacks, no pollution. The city fathers in that town had been careful all along its history.

Mike drove by the Stephen Decatur School and it was neat and orderly. Then he went back to a hotel just off the square.

The gray stone building was flush with the walk and there were bay windows on the corners up the whole three stories. He got one of those rooms.

He unpacked the car and carried all the army equipment up the stairs to the second floor. He made it without any particular weakness, and he knew he was healing. But he became still and waited to see if any of the splinters inside him had shifted. Would he always be so conscious of them?

He put his things away neatly. That was a drilled-in army habit of long standing. Then he mixed a drink and sat in the chair in the bay window and lit a cigarette.

After the long desert sojourn, he watched ordinary people with great appreciation. The time he'd spent in Germany hadn't satisfied that craving.

Mike watched as the people below him on the street walked freely, with direction, with purpose.

With all the turmoil in the world, with all the world trouble on the news, did Americans ever stop to think how fortunate they were? If they watched the news, they had to know.

With the tearing down of the Berlin Wall, the real surprise was to gradually realize the terrible time all those people behind the Iron Curtain had survived. And even with two generations of brutal suppression, the people still wanted freedom. They'd never given up.

Mike sipped his drink and lighted another cigarette. He was glad to be home. He was getting too old for the Rambo ramifications. He wanted... He wanted...

He wasn't sure what he wanted. Maybe when he was stronger and healed, he'd know.

When it was time to find something for supper, he dressed in slacks, shirt and casual jacket, with loafers. He went down to the lobby and asked the desk clerk to suggest a good place.

She sparkled at Mike and directed him to—the Greasy Spoon.

"Cholesterol?"

"It's an old place, dating from the nineteen forties. It's a joke."

Cautiously Mike inquired, "Does that include the food?"

"Try it."

"If I have a heart attack in twenty years, I'll be back."

"Or—" she smiled and blushed a little "—you could just . . . stay."

He almost smiled and touched one finger to his forehead as he left. He wondered how friendly she might be for a night or two . . . and if he . . . could.

The Greasy Spoon was diagonally across the square from the hotel, on a side street, and it was a clean, pleasant surprise. He had corned beef and cabbage that was superb. He could cut the corned beef with his fork. And he ended the meal with a strawberry trifle.

He sat back and sighed in his contentment, lighted a cigarette and found that life was good.

A woman at the next table covered her nose with her napkin and coughed in a very fake way, but she glared at him.

The waitress came over and said kindly, "This is a nonsmoking restaurant."

Mike looked at her blankly. Then he said, "Oh, sorry." And he looked for an ashtray. There was none.

The waitress said, "I'll take it."

He gave her the cigarette and watched her walk away with it. Then he looked at the woman and said to her, "Sorry."

She gave him a formal nod of acknowledgment for his apology but no smile.

Mike relaxed back in his chair, stubbornly in place. The old lady thought she'd won. He coughed into his hand.

Mike considered that the problem with the United States was that women were getting too strong. Men should never have allowed women to get the vote. That had been a serious mistake. Were they content with just voting? No. They were interfering with everything, but mostly they were interfering in men's lives.

When men were running the country, they could spit, smoke and scratch without even thinking about it. Now, along with all that, men were becoming more and more limited. They couldn't swat women on their bottoms or proposition them or fire them for being uncooperative. Women ruled.

If Iran could get the women out of schools and back into the veil in two weeks, then the American men should be able to do something similar in twenty-four hours.

Of course, women outnumbered men. That meant every man would have to take on a couple of women. Mike smiled. He could do that.

He got up from his chair and rummaged through his pockets for money. He left the tip and went over to the cash register. The slightly blushing waitress was there with his bill. She gave him a pack of cigarettes.

He shook his head chidingly.

Still blushing, with her body very aware of him, she said, "Our no-smoking sign needs to be larger. Of course—" she smiled a little more and her eyes danced wickedly "—you really ought not smoke."

He frowned a grin at her and scolded softly, "You, too?" And his tone was incredulous. Here was one of the women that he might convert.

As she rang up the sales, she inquired sassily, "Did that lady put those scratches on your face? Or are you just a contentious man?"

Deliberately underplaying it, he was surprised to find himself saying, "I got those in the Gulf." The fact that that statement would get her attention, and he'd used it deliberately, did amuse him. He'd seen all the yellow ribbons on all the fences and trees clear around the country, waiting for the troops to come home.

She handed Mike his change, as she teased, "The Gulf by Texas? A shark did that?"

And he watched himself in some shock, as he raised a kindly, gentle gaze to hers and said, "The Persian Gulf."

In a normal voice, she exclaimed, "You were *wounded?*"

Before he could take control, Mike said in an innocent expression of trust, "You should see the rest of my fragile body." And he licked his lips like a tomcat.

Her startled stare explored his face and then went down his body. She said, "Uhhh..."

He smiled a little and erased the whole drama by saying, "She had long fingernails."

Then the waitress didn't know what to think and she stood there, trying to decide, as he gave her a nod and walked out of the restaurant.

Mike walked along, disgruntled by his conduct. It probably came from being so long in a position of potential danger and not being able to do anything about it. First the long wait, then the fierce actual fight, which had been so shockingly destructive.

He'd never before thought of the enemy as being humans who lived and died. People who had had lives, just as he had. But he had survived. Was he suffering guilt for being alive? Is that why he was being so asinine?

And he thought maybe he should have been more receptive to the counseling offered. He should have listened. He might have adjusted better to returning to this untouched other side of the world.

He walked around a while in the coolness of the March evening. Then he went back to his room. Before he went to sleep, he took out the picture of the class and went over their names again. And that of Miss Benton. What was Miss Benton's first name?

Two

Standing in her empty classroom after the school day was over, thirty-five-year-old, and single, Sara Benton was a wreck. Who the *heck* would have thought Master Sergeant Michael Brown would come to see a third-grade class in Byford, Indiana? How *could* he show up there?

Even in that festering environment, rife with hot rumor, never had one gone throughout the entire school as fast as the fact that Sergeant Brown was coming there tomorrow! TOMORROW!

And all the teachers, and particularly the single ones, were giggly, breathless, chattering and carrying on in a completely disgraceful manner. Good grief! Just because an adult male who looked as if he might have all his juices intact was going to come to that school. They were all out-of-control. Frivolous. Silly.

Furiously Sara thought she was all that poor man had to protect him from being mobbed. She didn't want to be his ... protector! Darn it, anyway.

All of the classes had written the same kind of letters To Any Soldier, but only her—*their* Sergeant Brown had replied. Michael. He'd sent lots of pictures of the desert, how he lived, his sand-stained laundry on a rope, guys eating from containers that were called MRE and there had been two pictures ... of ... him.

The one on the bulletin board showed an anonymous soldier in full gear, his face shadowed by his helmet. He could be anyone. He was carrying a wicked rifle and had all sorts of paraphernalia hanging on him. She'd only put that one on the bulletin board because she had kept the other one.

She took the other one from her purse and looked at it. It was laminated so that the picture didn't betray how many times she'd taken it out and looked at it.

He was standing there without his helmet. He had his hands on his hips. He had a canteen and other things hanging off his belt. He was grinning, his eyelashes were down, almost covering his eyes and those eyes glinted in amusement over something. Something that was probably salacious. He looked that type.

For months, now, Sara had spent idle hours reforming him and changing him into a perfect man, gentle, considerate and madly in love with her. But did he have the sense to stay away from the school? No. He was coming there! She would meet him, he would dismiss her as an old maid and he would leave. All men left.

An intrusive voice demanded, "Sara! What are you going to wear tomorrow? Something from Frederick's of Hollywood?" Her friend Marilyn laughed and waved as she ducked back out the door.

Sara put her hand on her nice chest and took a calming breath. That's all she'd heard since his call to Mrs. Atwood that morning. All those silly, teasing comments had rattled Sara to the point that she would probably freeze up and not be able to appear calm and welcoming and function properly when he arrived ... tomorrow.

She had managed twice to say, "He's probably married. He likes kids, and not many single men would understand that kids are people, too."

And another of her friends had looked at the bulletin-board picture and said, "He doesn't wear a ring. He's not too young. He may be single and within a reasonable age range."

That had stunned Sara. All those single teachers thought Sergeant Brown was fair game ... for *them!*

That had made her indignant—for *him*—of course. He would be swamped by eager females. It would turn his head, and he wouldn't be able to see what an excellent person Sara Benton was.

Men were all alike. Women were given no other choice but those exceptionally flawed, only half-civilized creatures. Who else would trot off to the ends of the world to play at war?

Uhhh ... Women would.

There had been a good many women over there with those men in the Persian Gulf.

That thought did intrude. Sara's blue eyes frowned out the window to the playground.

Finally Sara decided that the government had probably sent the women along to be a counterbalance to the recklessness of the men. With women's cool heads, the conflict had lasted a remarkably brief time, for a war. Without them, the war would probably have dragged on for years and years, like Vietnam.

As it was, when Stormin' Norman wanted to keep going, it was probably a woman who had said, "That *is* enough!"

Without women, where would men be?

And one of that wild breed was coming there tomorrow. He wouldn't be tamed like Mr. Pearson. You wouldn't catch Tim Pearson going off to a battle of bombs and blood and dismem—all that awful stuff.

It was especially a surprise that Michael—Sergeant Brown was coming by at that time. They hadn't heard from him for a while. What had he been doing? He could have sent a postcard and explained himself to them.

Several times she'd dialed part of the 800 number to inquire about him. But since she might have had to explain exactly who she was and why she was calling, she'd never managed to complete the dialing.

He would be there. Tomorrow.

She looked at the room and thought it was hopelessly childish. What did she expect? It was a third-grade room. How adult were third graders? What impression did she want to make on him? She was the teacher of the class. That was all.

It had been the kids who'd wanted to write to a soldier, and Sara had found out the Persian Gulf military address so that they could. Not one child had been reluctant. Even the military nonconformist Teddy had written. But so had Melissa. That had surprised Sara. Melissa was such a snob, and a sergeant was not a commissioned officer. Melissa had mentioned that.

Mrs. Atwood came by Sara's room and asked, "Ready?"

My God! He was there? Sara gasped and put her hand to her throat.

"Did I startle you? I am sorry. Almost everyone is gone."

"I was trying to decide if I should change the lesson plan for tomorrow, so that the children could show off a little." Then Sara added in clarification: "Tomorrow. For Sergeant Brown."

"I would imagine that he will only be here for a short time," Mrs. Atwood cautioned. "He will probably be anxious to get on to see his family."

In spite of her daydreams, Sara was forced to face that. His . . . family. Yes. He probably did have a family. But why would a man who had a family leave them and go off to war? How rude he was. Sara said coolly, "You're probably right."

Mrs. Atwood urged, "Come along. You can walk me to my car."

"Is there some problem?"

"No. I just want to be sure you leave the building."

"Why?"

"So you don't spend the night cleaning your room and being sure each child has a drawing on the board so that Sergeant Brown can see it. How would you handle one of Teddy's drawings? Write a dissertation explaining it, to put alongside it?"

Sara smiled, then laughed and said, "Teddy." She shook her head slowly.

Mrs. Atwood pronounced, "Every mother's dream. Every teacher's nightmare."

"Yes."

"Come along."

Her insistence irked Sara. Mrs. Atwood treated her as if she hadn't the brains to know when it was time to go home. It was only— It was almost five.

"Don't come too early in the morning. Mr. Jamison would be annoyed, and we need him."

Mr. Jamison was the custodian.

Sara looked around the room, put on her coat and picked up her purse. "I'll be here at the regular time."

"So will I. I am simply dying to see this Sergeant Brown. He wrote his letters to the children in such a way that he must be familiar with ones who are this age. He was kind to write to them."

As they left her room, Sara mentioned, "Someone had written to a major magazine's Letters to the Editor and said how much all the people in the Persian Gulf had enjoyed the school kids' letters. And the writer said it was possible that not all of them would be answered, but the kids needed to know how much all the guys had appreciated the mail."

"I saw that."

"Michael wrote to us."

Mrs. Atwood was conscious that Sara had called the sergeant Michael. "Yes. It will be interesting to see him in person."

"If he wrote to us, he would have written to his family, too," Sara declared with confidence. "The pictures were especially interesting ... for the kids." Sara clutched her purse closely in a white-knuckled hand, as if a suspicious Mrs. Atwood would snatch it from her and find Michael's picture hidden there.

They had reached the parking lot, and only their two patient cars were there. Mrs. Atwood smiled kindly. "Would you like to come home with me? Glenn will have supper about ready. We'd love your company."

"Why, thank you, but not tonight."

"Then I'll see you in the morning. Not too early."

"No, of course not. 'Bye." Sara was brisk and businesslike as she got into her car and closed the door. Then she had to open her purse to get her car keys out. She glanced casually over to see if Mrs. Atwood had field glasses and was checking to see what was in her purse... like the picture of Michael.

Great Caesar's ghost, Sara thought in shock, she had to be slipping a cog. What had happened to the cool, collected, disciplined teacher, Sara Benton? She had to regain control and be normal. What was normal?

With her mind nicely diverted from the cause of her being perturbed, Sara drove home. Home was a small, two-bedroom house on the outskirts of Byford. She lived alone.

Beyond her backyard was a scraggly woodlot. In another month there would be violets scattered there, poking up through the dead leaves under the trees. She would climb over the inadequate fence and pick bouquets to take to school.

She parked her car precisely and went into her house. She was terminally neat. Even on her deathbed she would straighten the covers. She put her coat into the closet and set her purse on the hall table.

She looked at herself in the mirror above the table and decided that she was not unattractive. She was five feet four inches and she exercised enough that her figure was trim. Her posture was good and her complexion smooth. Maybe she was a little plain. Her hair was a plain brown, but her eyes were brilliantly blue.

Sara went into her bedroom and opened her closet. She pushed some of the clothes aside and considered the blue dress that hung there. She'd bought it last fall at a sale in Fort Wayne's enormous Glenbrook Mall.

The dress was the color of her eyes. The neck of the dress was a little low. She lifted the hanger from the bar and held the dress against her, glancing into the full-length mirror on the inside of the closet door. It was a magic dress. She would wear it the next day.

She was so distracted from her routine that for supper she ate a peanut-butter sandwich while she was standing in the kitchen looking blindly out her back window.

That evening, in succession, she had seven phone calls from other teachers asking inane things like: "What do you think he'll be like?" and "Can you believe he'd actually come here?" and "Aren't you curious?" and "He might be a dud. You can't really see his face in that picture on your bulletin board."

And with those calls, Sara knew that she would not wear the blue dress the next day. She could not. Everyone would think she was trying to lure Michael Brown, who probably had a family somewhere else.

Sara was not a home-wrecker.

She felt depressed that she would not get to wear the magic blue dress. So. What would she wear?

She took the phone off the hook and went back to her closet. She spent almost an hour, during which she discarded the possibility of wearing anything she owned. Did that mean she would go to school in her black satin-and-lace slip? It was a temptation.

She finally got out her old brown skirt and a boy's brown long-sleeved shirt. She felt her mouth pull down and that annoyed her. She was not trying to seduce Michael Brown. Well, maybe being a "Brown," he'd be susceptible to the color? Hardly.

He probably liked red.

She didn't own one red garment except for a garter belt that she'd never worn. She'd won it playing bridge three years before at Cindy's shower.

She considered having owned that belt for three years. And she thought maybe tomorrow would be the day to initiate the new Sara. She would wear the brown skirt and shirt, but she would also wear the red garter belt. While no one else would know she wore it, she would know.

She studied herself and found that, except for her blue eyes, she looked a whole lot like a wren. What woman wants to look like a bird?

She pulled her hair back and considered her forehead. It was really quite nice. She would change her hairstyle. She showered, washing her hair, and combed it back and blew it dry with her hair dryer. It looked free.

She looked a little reckless. She looked like a woman who would secretly wear a red garter belt. She smiled a mysterious smile and gave herself a slow wink.

She was becoming peculiar from living alone.

So. She'd say to Mike, "How about moving in?"

And watching her face in the mirror, she wondered what he would have to say about that? The very idea of moving in with the brown wren, Sara Benton, would probably terrify him.

The new Sara went to bed nude. She got up about fifteen minutes later and put on her nightgown. A woman can't break all her old habits in one day. Then she crawled back into bed and went to sleep.

The next morning, a lot of people in Byford woke up with Michael Brown on their minds. One of the people at the local television station had been alerted by Mrs. Atwood.

Sara new that all the kids would be excited, but she didn't know about all the others who were also excited. The desk clerk at the hotel had called, "Good morning" to an early rising Mr. Brown. The waitress in the Greasy Spoon had served Mike breakfast and was torn between flirting and being careful of a man who said he'd been scratched up by a woman.

She saw that he watched the time and ate with dispatch. He left another generous tip and paid at the cash register. He gave her a quick, serious wink that meant nothing and he left.

Mike went back to the hotel and up to his room, taking the stairs but going slowly. He then set about dressing up in the combat uniform and assembling the gear that he'd worn in the Persian Gulf.

The material of his uniform was camouflaged in desert colors of browns and sand. So was his helmet. His trouser bottoms were tucked into the tops of his sturdy dark boots, which came up to his calves.

He picked up the web belt with suspenders that were heavily padded. And the rucksack was attached to the back of the suspenders. In combat it would contain three days' supply of clean clothing and one MRE container. There was a chemical protection suit that would be included.

Suspended from the belt would be two ammo pouches and an entrenching tool—as the shovel was called—and a full canteen. There would be a chemical decontamination kit, to wash off his skin, and two filled syringes to counteract chemicals.

There would be a chemical-protection mask that would be fastened from his belt with straps around his leg and up over his shoulder. It would be almost impossible to lose it.

His camouflaged helmet wasn't metal. It was plastic and was molded into one unit. The webbing around his head was built into the helmet and was unremovable. Unlike the army helmet of World War II, a man couldn't cook or carry water in the new helmet. The army wanted their people to wear the helmets.

As required, Mike had turned in his M-16 rifle, so he carried no gun. He carried his gear and was surprisingly quiet, but he looked formidable.

He checked out of the hotel and paid his bill before he drove to the school.

Mrs. Atwood had suggested that he arrive about nine that morning. And being prompt and disciplined, he did arrive on the dot.

He eased out of his car and removed the equipment he'd brought along. He turned toward the school building. It looked like about any school. It was quiet. He then noted that some kids were in the windows and pointing at him. He walked up the sidewalk to the entrance.

A grinning woman awaited him. She pushed open the door, and he took it from her hand. She moved back, saying, "I would guess you're Michael Brown."

"You got it right."

"I'm the principal, Mrs. Atwood. I spoke to you yesterday. Would you mind terribly if later this morning we'd have a general assembly, so that the rest of the kids can see you?"

Good God, what had he gotten himself into? Her saying "a little later" made it sound as if this would be longer than the fifteen minutes he'd planned. "No. That would be all right."

"We'd just so appreciate it."

He nodded seriously. "Which way is Miss Benton's room?"

"Right this way. They're so excited."

They could hear him coming. His equipment made odd little sounds. His steps weren't a civilian's. Now how could that be different? Sara's breaths picked up and only her deadly glances kept the kids from rushing to the door and screaming.

Sara turned, just as he filled the door. He was still in combat dress. Obviously, he'd left the battlefield and come straight there! Sara was overwhelmed.

She opened her mouth and the kids all stood up and just cheered. It was charming. They smiled and lifted both their hands and yelled.

He coughed and smiled and came into the room. He was so touched. He could feel moisture in his eyes and he coughed again. He looked at the teacher... *and there she was!*

She was there! He was stunned by her and he wanted to just stare. He stood immobilized.

She said, "Hello." She could actually speak. She smiled. "I'm Sara Benton." She was being carefully formal with him.

The kids were still standing, grinning, silent.

He nodded to the prim Sara Benton then looked at the kids, and he knew them. Pointing them out, he said, "Jeannie, Bill, George, Mattie, Nancy, John One aanndd—" he stretched, searching "—there's John Two, Teddy, Melissa—" And he named them all.

"Well, Sara Benton, where's Jimmy?" He said that as if she were hiding Jimmy.

He'd said her name! She smiled and smiled, and her tongue finally kicked in and said, "He was transferred."

"Tell him I asked after him."

And she blushed furiously and smiled widely and replied, "I will." Then her tongue went on and blurted, "What happened to your face?"

"Shrapnel." He was soothed by her shock. He looked at the kids, and being a disciplined military man, he treated the kids as he would his troops. He said, "You may sit down."

They sat, folded their hands on their desk and kept their eyes on him and smiled.

Sara was impressed.

Teddy said, "See our board with your pictures?"

Miss Benton chided, "Teddy."

Mike nodded, then said, "If you have questions, raise your hand. You get one each. No repeats. Understand? Think it out first."

Miss Benton was *very* impressed.

And Mike said, "Maybe you'd be interested in all this gear I'm carrying. I can't wear it right now—I was wounded. On my body there're more cuts like those on my face."

And he said, "I'm still a little wobbly, do you mind if I sit down?"

Sara got her chair and started to lift it, but he reached and effortlessly took it from her. He set it at the front of the room, facing the kids, and he did sit down.

She asked, "Are you all right?"

He turned his head and gave her a quick wink.

That could mean anything.

He went right ahead, taking over like the macho man he was, not asking if there was anything Miss Benton wanted to say or have him do or whatever. He sat there and undid and took out things and showed them. He listed the equipment he didn't have with him. He explained why he'd needed those items. The reasons were serious. But the kids laughed that MRE meant Meal Ready to Eat.

Sara knew the MRE would be taken home, by the kids, and their use of it would drive their parents all crazy.

Then Mike told the kids. "And here is my rucksack." He took out a roll of papers that held their letters and the two class pictures. Very seriously, he thanked them for writing to him.

They loved him. And Sara decided she'd lure him away from his wife and children and keep him. He was so precious, so great with the kids and so gorgeously male.

And he looked over at her and riveted her with one look. He scared her stomach and shivered her bones and thrilled her skin. She became a little pale and didn't say anything.

The questions the kids asked were about what was expected. They mostly just wanted his attention.

"Were you scared?"

"Yes."

"Did it hurt when you were hurt?"

"Yeah."

"Does it still hurt?"

"Some. I'm on leave until I heal better. I had to carry this gear because if I wore it, it would rub or

press down on some of the places where I was hit."
And he got sympathetic sounds from them.

When Teddy's turn came, he smiled at Mike and
said, "I brought a friend to see you."

Mike was cautious. "Oh?"

And Sara knew that he was married. Only married
people or teachers knew to be that cautious with children.

"Wanna see him?"

"Maybe."

See? He was no fool. Sara asked, "What is it,
Teddy?"

"I'll show him. May I?"

Sara looked at Mike and he gave a minimal nod.

Sara gave permission. "All right, Teddy, but be
brief."

He rose carefully, holding his stomach and went to
Mike whose eyes began to show his amusement. He
was a man who'd been raised with a slew of kids, and
he wasn't surprised when Teddy unbuttoned his shirt
at the waist and took out a mouse.

Bedlam began. Mike laughed the most marvelous
low male laughter, and Teddy laughed with him. Kids
yelled questions and were supplied with the answer
and some of the little girls screamed. Melissa was a
screamer.

Sara was firm. She commanded order. And she got
it! She then looked at Teddy and took a breath.

But Mike said, "Thank you for showing me your
mouse. In the desert, some of the guys adopted rats
and made pets of them."

There was interest and some disgust from the
watchers.

Mike handled the mouse and declared it healthy and a nice pet. Teddy glowed. Mike asked, "How are you going to get him home?"

Teddy shrugged and considered.

Mike suggested, "We could put him in my ruck-sack. He'd be safe there."

And Teddy agreed to it.

Sara viewed Mike as a brilliant man who knew children. How did he know them so well? And her stomach knotted over the fact that in all probability he really was married.

All too soon, Mrs. Atwood called on the intercom and asked if ten o'clock would be okay for everyone to gather in the auditorium.

Sara replied kindly, "Yes. We've been a bit delayed."

Having Miss Benton's agreement, there was then an intercom announcement to all the classrooms about the assembly.

Sara had kids lined up to go to the rest rooms and meet again in the hall.

Sara said to Mike, "If you'd like to use the teacher's rest room, Herbert can lead you there. It's just down the hall."

Mike opened his mouth to say that he could manage to find a rest room by himself, but he glanced down at Herbert who was earnest, and he just said, "Thank you."

Sara then said, "I'll lock the door so your things will be safe here."

He repeated gravely, "Thank you."

Following the earnest Herbert, Mike considered that Miss Benton was prissy and she might not be at all suitable. He wanted a woman who would fly in the face of convention and be free. He wasn't sure that she had the sand for it.

When they met again in the hall, Miss Benton said, "At the assembly, would you please thank all the kids for the letters they wrote to the Persian Gulf? All the grades wrote letters, as we wrote to you, but only you replied."

He gave one nod.

Herbert then escorted Mike to Mrs. Atwood while the rest of his class filed into the auditorium and took seats in their assigned area.

Mike carried a chair up onto the stage, placed it in the middle and sat down.

When Mike stood up and introduced himself, Sara knew he could control even Mrs. Atwood.

The entire assembly stood and cheered.

Mike bowed formally, then he sat down. He sat there with his knees wide, one fist on his hip and the other hand was spread with his thumb on the outside of his thigh. He moved his eyes, looking at them all. Then he nodded and held up a hand for silence.

Three

The excited rustle in the audience stilled and the only sounds were the whispers of the slight movements the audience made in order to stretch to see Mike.

The lights were on, on the stage, and the TV camera was unobtrusively set up at the back. They had a zoom lens. They taped the entire sequence.

When everyone had settled down, Mike said very seriously, "I came here to tell you that all your letters were read." He looked for Miss Benton and found her standing along the wall to his right. "Some of the letters were passed on to other guys that didn't get any mail. If nobody told you how much it meant to them to get the letters, it's because they all thought somebody else had written and told you that your letters meant a lot to all of us. Thank you." He glanced again at Miss Benton.

Those gathered in the auditorium grinned and clapped, and over by the wall Miss Benton's heart melted. He'd done that for her. She'd asked, and he'd responded perfectly.

Mike then said, "If you have any questions, hold up your hand and I'll try to answer them." Then he elaborated: "I won't answer the hand, I'll answer the question."

Even that got a laugh.

Some of the questions were very thoughtful, most were just vocal exuberance. One young female teacher asked The Question: "Are you married?"

And the other teachers and the older kids all laughed.

Mike grinned and said, "No." But his glance didn't linger on the questioner, he immediately looked and pointed to another.

Sara was riveted. He was not married! He wasn't. She should have worn the blue dress instead of this brown wren combination. However, maybe a dress didn't matter. He had looked away from Sheila, who had unbuttoned the next two buttons on her high-necked blouse before she'd asked if he was married. And even with Sara wearing the wren outfit he'd given her that riveting look, when he couldn't possibly have known that she was wearing a red garter belt.

Mike was saying that war was a terrible thing. Thinking people only resorted to fighting for a very serious reason. It had to be worth the lives that would be lost in any war.

And someone asked, "How were you wounded?"

"Shrapnel is the splattering of metal slivers. It's not nice." He stood up in order to carefully ease his shirt from his pants, then he unbuttoned his shirt down to the waist—leaving the bottom of the shirt still buttoned.

He told them, "I'm just showing you the top half." He said that seriously, so no one giggled or smirked as he eased the shirt from his shoulders and allowed it to hang from his waist. Then he turned to allow them to see the damage done to him. A couple of the surgical intrusions were still bandaged.

There was a whisper of breaths indrawn, but the witnesses didn't comment. What could they say?

In that silence, Mike put his arms back into his sleeves and pulled the shirt carefully up over his shoulders. He again buttoned it, but he left the tails outside his trousers. In that same earnest way, he said, "And you're looking at a guy who won, who's walking around. War is a terrible thing."

Sara had been surprised by his display, but his following words had more impact, then, than any other way they could have been said.

He hadn't known he would face a full school assembly. Mrs. Atwood had surprised him with that, Sara knew. For Mike to make this point so dramatically was done on an earnest impulse.

They were all sobered. He had been hurt. He could have been one of those killed. And the lost and wounded ones came into their minds and became more precious.

After Mike was again seated, one of the hands was pointed to and the kid said, "My uncle wasn't hurt."

And Mike replied, "Thank God."

Questions continued but they became repetitious, with kids only wanting to be singled out. Mike smiled at Mrs. Atwood. "Enough?"

She agreed. "Enough."

She thanked him for coming and allowed the audience to give Mike one more rousing cheer, then she dismissed the assembly.

Herbert came for Mike and importantly took him back to the classroom another way so that they didn't have to go through the crowded halls. After seeing Mike's back and arms, Mrs. Atwood couldn't allow him to be unknowingly jostled or hurt.

When Sara got back to the room, Herbert and Mike were waiting by the locked door. Kids were calling to Mike and reaching to just touch him. No touch was more than feather-light. It was charming to see the children's compassion.

Sara unlocked the door, and the lined-up kids went inside. She said to her guest, "You were magnificent."

He blinked and looked unknowing and puzzled by her. That could have been when she really fell in love with him. She'd been in love with the idea of a man, now it was the man, himself. That made her feel poignant, because she knew such love would be unrequited.

She also knew her posturings and musings were all utter nonsense. No normal person falls in love on such a brief meeting. Just because he could handle kids, and was injured from being in a faraway war, and he looked like a wicked dream, was not enough reason to decide she loved him. She was a mature woman of thirty-five and she had put all that nonsense past her.

Not only that, but he couldn't possibly be interested—except for that one look. Maybe he was a lecher. Maybe he wasn't particular and was just interested in whatever happened to be available. She would have to be distant and cool.

But she could be kind. He had been injured, and he had written back when the kids needed to feel involved with the men in the war. He had done that. And it had been important to the kids.

Teddy went to the rucksack. His mouse was still there, and Teddy put the mouse back inside his shirt.

Watching Teddy do that, Sara stiffened slightly and all her surface skin shivered in revulsion.

Mike observed, "You don't like mice."

She replied, "No."

Since she didn't elaborate or flirt or shiver to entice his glance, he knew she really did not like mice and was being very brave. "I'll take Teddy home at noon and he can leave the mouse there."

"I'll call his mother to see if that's okay. I'll have to go along. I'm responsible for the boy."

"I understand. Little boys have never appealed to me. They're generally a nuisance."

She didn't realize he was reassuring her and took him literally. She identified the nuisance: "Teddy."

"Yep. You can tell one a mile away."

And Sara knew that the reason Mike recognized the rascally Teddy was that it takes one to know one... unless one is a teacher. Teachers know at first sight any rascally males who have the potential of being a nuisance.

She looked at Mike with measuring eyes. He was one. And being a grown one, he was dangerous for an adult female.

Her skin prickling, then, was of an entirely different kind than that caused by seeing a mouse. The different feeling was the strange and scary shivering in her body that was exciting.

Having obtained permission all the way around, Sara went with Mike to take Teddy and his mouse home. She had an allotted twenty minutes for lunch. Mike carried his gear out to his car. As they did that, he noticed that Miss Benton had on high heels and her quick steps made her chest jiggle in a very eye-catching way. He put Teddy into the backseat, carefully helped Miss Benton to sit in front, and Mike drove.

Teddy's mother was about as excited as all the single teachers had been, and she never even glanced at Sara, but she *had* briefly noticed her own son. However, she then saw the mouse and she screeched like a banshee. She hadn't known he had a mouse.

It was only then Sara realized that little fact. Sara had just asked if they could drive Teddy home to leave his pet there. And Teddy's mother had replied a rather vague, "Yes."

Teddy's mother didn't want the mouse in the house. Sara could understand that.

Neither Mike nor Teddy understood. They tried to reason with the obstinate woman, but she was firm.

Mike inquired, "Didn't you know?"

"No." While Teddy's mother hadn't known about the mouse, she did know that she didn't want the creature in her house.

Teddy was a little forlorn, and Mike advised, "Next time, get permission."

Teddy wobbled his head in a nothing reply to that.

Somehow Sara knew it wouldn't be long before Teddy had another secret pet. What would be next? He'd only promised not to get another mouse. Teachers know about being specific.

So then the only thing they could do was go to Sara's house. There they called several people to try to find someone who would harbor a pet mouse. It wasn't easy. There was none.

While Sara slapped together some sandwiches and poured out glasses of milk, Mike went through the Byford phone book and made some calls. He called the television station and talked to the cameraman who'd filmed the assembly at the Stephen Decatur Elementary School. The cameraman declined the mouse.

Sara called the school office and said she might be a little late. The response was noncommittal.

They found that no one wanted a mouse. Not even the veterinarian.

Sara suggested letting it go in a field.

Teddy was appalled. "He's a house mouse."

With no other alternative, they put the mouse in an old bird cage that Sara had bought at a garage sale on impulse one time and had hung amid some plants as a decoration.

"A bird cage?" Mike questioned that. He hadn't questioned Teddy having a mouse, but he obviously thought a bird cage was a little quirky. Especially since she didn't have a bird.

And he walked around and looked into her rooms and asked, "Who else lives here?"

She said, "No one."

"Just you?"

"If no one lives here—"

And he said, "Yeah."

The errant trio got back to the school after classes had reconvened.

"You don't *have* to come inside," Sara assured Mike with considerable reluctance.

But if he didn't, he wouldn't have any reason to see her again, so being an army man, he said, "I need to. You two might be in hot water, and they won't scold you when I'm there to hear. My 'hero' facade ought to last through the afternoon, before Mrs. Atwood realizes I'm just an ordinary man."

Teddy laughed aloud, and Sara gave Mike a disbelieving stare, but she couldn't argue with the fact that having him along would indeed be a buffer to a stony and cool silence.

They went inside the empty hall and to Sara's room. Sara walked in first and her hurried steps in those high heels caused her bottom to shiver. She entranced Mike.

Mrs. Atwood, herself, was directing the class. The kids were reading silently, and Mrs. Atwood was just a bit terse. However, as Mike came into the room following the tardy two, Mrs. Atwood smiled benignly and turned the room back to Sara.

As she left, Mrs. Atwood again thanked Mike for visiting their school.

He was polite.

He spent the afternoon sitting in one of the small chairs at the back of the room. He was tired and his body was not too comfortable. His eyes dulled and the white lines around his mouth showed that he was in pain. He toughed it out.

Sara was acutely aware of him. She felt his eyes on her and she was so conscious of him that she got a headache. How could she be so immature as to get a headache because a man was sitting in the back of her room and she was in full view?

And she realized she wasn't that immature. The reason her head hurt was because she'd changed her hairstyle and the hair roots were objecting to having to lie in a different direction.

What in life wasn't contrary? Why did she have to endure irritable hair roots? With all the things in the world to cope with, why hair roots? She felt she just might dye them all purple and see what they'd have to say about that. The roots would probably reject the dye and she'd end up bald on top.

End up bald on top? How droll. And she suddenly remembered a cadence spelling joke about Archibald—what had it been? Something Irish? An Irish name. And she had been so distracted by the telling of it, in a cadenced repetition, that she hadn't realized until years later that the whole thing had been blatantly vulgar and extremely insulting to women.

She cast a censoring glance back to Mike. Her eyes rested on his face. He was drowsing. He looked very tired. Why was he sticking around?

And it came to her. He probably had no place to go.

She was stunned by the knowledge. A wounded hero, home from the war, on convalescent leave with no place to go. Oh, the poor, dear man. Were the third graders at Stephen Decatur Elementary School his only family?

That was impossible.

So when they were outside at recess, with the kids running around and yelling, showing off for Mike, she asked, "Were you an orphan?"

And he was surprised. "How did you know that?"

With tender compassion, she asked, "Have you no family?"

He stared at her, his mind rushing and clicking with a speed a computer could envy. "No relatives." That was honest. Only a portion of the Brown hoard were actual kin to one another. He licked his lips.

"Where will you stay tonight?"

"Oh." He looked off to the side so she couldn't see his eyes glint. "I'll sleep in my car. My pay hasn't caught up with me, since I've been moving around. It's not too bad. The passenger seat lies back and it's reasonable." Then he added the zinger, "I've gotten used to it again."

She was stunned.

So he said, "Would you mind if I had a shower at your place? It's been a long, warm day. I'll sleep better, relaxed with a hot shower." Then he added, "There's not much water in the desert. We haven't had the luxury of water."

That was the killer. How could she refuse him? "Of course."

He didn't dare to ask what she was agreeing about. He'd just play it by ear and assume she meant to house him. If he worked it right, he could move in with her.

The day did end. The kids were comfortable with Mike and had accepted him as theirs. Actually, in another way, so had Sara. She felt responsible for him.

They left Sara's room with the exodus, and everyone called to Mike as they went through the halls to their cars. Driving ahead of Mike, Sara was a superb, careful leader, who dawdled, being sure he could follow her. They went to her house.

She would feed him supper. She decided that without any real conscious decision. It was uncanny. She was watching the rearview mirror so that she knew Mike wasn't lost and her mind was sorting through the available food in her refrigerator and freezer.

As they entered the house, she was a little animated to have him there and alone.

He asked in a draggy voice, "Would it be all right if I lie down for a little while?"

"Oh . . . yes, of course."

"It's been a long day." He played his trump: "I haven't been out of the hospital very long."

"Yes. Are you faint?"

"Naw." He lifted his hand and his head went down to meet his fingertips. It was beautifully subtle. He'd seen a guy do that once in front of an aloof nurse, and Mike had scorned such antics with an inward sneer. But he'd learned quickly that a smart man could learn a lot by simple observation.

She said compassionately, "We need to get your boots off. You can lie down in the other room."

He demurred. "The sofa will be okay." He lifted his head to glance at it, and it was as he recalled, a two-seater. He had her.

"It's too short."

"I don't like to be a nuisance."

"You aren't. I can't tell you how important it was to the children to get your letters. To write back to you. To have all the pictures. You've been wonderful. Come, let me help you."

"Okay." He made his voice a little faint.

"Should I call my doctor?"

"No, no, not now. I just need to lie down for a while."

"I should have made you stay here at noon. I'd seen how badly you'd been hurt. Can you make it by yourself?" She watched him anxiously.

"If I could put my arm over your shoulder?"

"Oh, yes. Would it hurt if I put my arm around your waist?"

"My belt protected my waist. You can do that okay."

She helped him and was very earnest and concerned. He had to bite his lower lip to keep his Cheshire grin concealed.

She glanced up, saw him biting his lip and thought he was in pain. She was appalled. "Oh, Mike—"

"I'm okay."

He was so brave that a tear leaked from her eye.

He saw her tenderhearted tear and his conscience did twinge a little, but he had to bite into his lip a little harder to stop his goatish snort.

"Sit there until I turn back the bed covers. Is it too cool in here?"

He was in a sexual sweat. "No."

The seat of the elaborate little needlepointed overstuffed chair was so short that it hit him just above midcalf. "I'd break the chair if I sat on it."

"No. It's very sturdy. Ladies weighed more then. Either that or their layers of clothing did."

Gingerly he sat down. And the chair did hold him. He leaned to unlace his high boots.

"Wait. I can help you. Just let me get the bed ready."

He looked at her busy body, her efficient attack on the bed and her jiggling breasts. He closed his eyes, but they popped back open. Then he looked at the pristine bed sheets. They were cotton and they'd been carefully ironed. "I ought to shower. That bed's clean and I'm not especially."

"I can change it for you later."

His nerves danced. If she changed it "later," then she expected him to need the bed later and he was going to spend the night? She expected him to? Ahhh... It was working. Or did she mean she'd change it after he left?

His computer mind whirled and clicked. "Do you want me to feed the mouse for you?" His voice was considerate and sincere.

She froze, mid-smoothing, and looked at him. "I'd forgotten the mouse. What are we going to do about it?"

She'd included him. They were partners in this. He asked with earnest candor, "Flush it?"

She was shocked. "What would Teddy say?"

"We'd tell him it got away."

"He'd know." She was stark.

"I'll tell him for you." He'd have to stay around to do that. "I'll do the flushing."

She plumped the pillows and then came to him and knelt before him to attack his boots. "You can't just ... drown it."

It was now his responsibility. "Mice swim." And he was reasonable. "They can't all live. We'd be knee-deep in mice. Did you see CNN's filming of the Australian mice that one year? Two men lifted a sheet of tin and exposed a couple hundred mice that ran in a wave, toward the camera, around the bottom of a pole. On top of the pole was a cat who watched very alertly, but from a safe distance."

"Only men would lift a concealment and expose all those mice. Ugh."

"You were very brave to allow Teddy to think you'd find that mouse a home."

She was distressed. "I must. How could I not?"

"Tell him there was a traveling salesman at the hotel who—"

"What would I be doing at the hotel?"

True. "Uh—"

"Lift your foot."

He did, and she pulled off the boot with some effort.

She said, "How can you lift your feet wearing those boots? Those weigh a ton!"

"But they cross deserts and rocks and protect the feet from dropped things like hammers or sheets of metal that reveal a hidden swarm of mice."

"Let's not talk about mice."

"Have you fed . . . our guest?"

"No. I'm trying to get you undressed so you can rest for a while."

"I'll help."

"I can't have you struggling with these boots."

"I'm used to them."

He took off the other one with such alacrity that she was impressed. And a niggle of doubt crept into her mind, that maybe he wasn't as frail as she'd thought. She watched him with some caution.

He was instantly aware of the change in her attitude. He faltered. He paused and hid his eyes with his lashes deliberately. He breathed through his mouth slowly.

"Are you okay?"

"Sure."

"I can undo buttons. I may not be able to handle those boots, but I can do buttons."

He leaned back slowly and gave her his arm.

She did those busily, then walked on her knees to the other side and did the other arm. Then she leaned up and began on his shirtfront.

He watched her face avidly. His breathing changed and he began to tremble.

She sympathized: "Oh. They should never have let you out of the hospital this soon. You're not strong enough. Shame on them. I thought the army took better care of their own."

"Well—" the army was big enough to handle contrived guilt "—there were a lot of guys hurt."

She eased the shirt off his shoulders with great care. "Can you stand up okay?"

He couldn't let her take off his pants. "I can handle that." And he waited for her to insist.

She said, "All right. Are you taking any medication?"

"Occasional aspirin."

"You'd think they could do better for you than that. But if you aren't taking any medication, you could have some wine."

"No beer?"

"I could go get some?"

"No, a glass of wine would be fine." And he expected, and was braced for, a ladies' sweet wine.

She went to fetch it, and he slowly unzipped his fly and eased out the bottom of his shirt. He emptied his pockets and put his wallet and cigarettes on the bedside table. Then he got out of his trousers and stood there in cotton army undershorts.

His body was good. The army saw to it they worked hard. They exercised hard. He was in good shape. He wasn't yet at the peak of his maturity. He was only thirty-six. A woman's physical peak is at age forty. At that time she can look any age. But a man was his most formidable at fifty. And Mike would be something to see at that age.

He knew he looked good and he was delaying, so that she could come in and see him. But he heard her talking to someone and he thought it prudent to get into bed. He needed her to think he should be there, and he needed any intruder to see he'd gained a foothold in her house.

She came in with the wine and said, "I've convinced my doctor to stop in and see you. He had a boy in my class last year, and he knows you're in town. The whole town knows. But he will come and see if he can make you more comfortable."

Good God. No way. "I'm okay. I'll see him tomorrow. Cancel him coming over."

"Are you sure?"

"Yeah. These cuts aren't new. There's really not much he could do unless some of the slivers move."

"Oh, Michael—" She couldn't think what to say to this wounded warrior. "Try this." She gave him a fragile crystal ladies' wineglass with a pale liquid floating inside it.

Knowing full well how that thimbleful would taste, he sipped it. It was ambrosia. It slid over his tongue like a balm, like a woman's gentle hand on a man's hot forehead, like cool water on a burning desert like last summer for Desert Shield. He was amazed. He licked his lips in savoring.

She explained, "Tim Pearson brought that over one time. He's a very civilized man. And he knows wines very well. How do you like it?"

"It's okay." Who was this . . . Tim Pearson?

"Are you hungry?"

"Yeah."

"Good. That's a good sign. Could you eat a steak?"

"Don't go to any trouble."

She smiled. "How do you like it?"

"Seared."

"Good grief." She was disgusted.

"Really. Get the griddle really hot and make the outside crusty."

She looked at the ceiling and threw out her arms. "A mouse in a bird cage, and a man who eats bloody raw meat."

He comforted her earnestly. "It shows you can adjust." He would bet Tim Pearson ate his meat welldone. "Does Pearson like his meat well-done?"

"Medium. And he eats with a knife and fork."

"So do I!" He was just a tad belligerent.

"I didn't say you didn't!"

She looked sassy. He knew what to do with sassy women. He took another sip of the wine. It was excellent. He contrived to look thoughtful, as he considered the taste.

The bed was comfortable. The room was a perfect temperature for a man home from the desert and into the cool of the Midwest spring.

He lay back and watched her as she straightened his clothing, hanging the pieces on hangers and putting them into the closet. She was so busy, so earnest, so concerned for him. A glow started in his heart.

He reached for his cigarettes on the bedside table. All day he hadn't been able to smoke but twice in the teachers' lounge and in his car on the way to Sara's house. He gave the pack a practiced joggle and lifted the pack to his mouth to take the exposed cigarette.

From the back of the pack, he took out a folder of matches and glanced up into her horrified face.

"You can't smoke!"

"My lungs don't leak."

"No. But you can't smoke. I'm allergic to smoke."

She was serious. He was stunned.

Four

Starkly Mike looked at Sara, but his response was automatic, "Then, I won't smoke."

In agitation, Sara protested, "I can't insist that you change. I know how addicted people get to cigarettes."

"I'll quit."

"I could get you a room at the hotel."

He sure as hell didn't want that! "I won't smoke," he repeated. "And we can pretend this is a hotel. In a hotel we could have rooms side by side. And I'll lock my door, so I'll be safe."

Safe? The phone rang, and she left the room to answer it.

He lifted the cigarette and looked at it. Then he put it under his nose and inhaled deeply. The things a man was forced to do, by circumstances and beyond his own profound awe, were never really appreciated.

She came back into the room and caught him smelling the tobacco. "You have a real addiction."

"No." He was impressed he got the actual word said.

"With all the rest of the things you must endure, I can't make you quit. Could you go out on the porch to smoke?"

"I suppose I could if I get the shakes."

She was stunned. "You're *that* addicted?"

"No. I was teasing you."

"Well, it really *would* be better for you, and for your healing wounds, if you could quit. I'll get you some gum."

How like a nonsmoker to think gum was a substitute for nicotine. He wondered if she could handle him chewing tobacco. It would be spitting that would be the problem, and he sure as hell couldn't swallow it. He sighed.

She was watching him kindly. "You're going to be on the TV news tonight. They're doing a special segment on you."

"Good God."

"You were brilliant. You did and said everything just right. You could get a copy of the tape." Saying that, she knew she would keep her own VCR copy.

Mike knew that Salty would like seeing it. Felicia would find it tame, but she loved him so much that she'd be pleased. "I suppose."

"You might have children . . . or do you?"

"Not that I know."

She was shocked. "What do you mean, 'Not that you know!'"

"It's an automatic male reply that doesn't mean anything."

"Well, it *sounds* as if—"

"I don't have any kids. I've never been married. I'm a career army man."

She studied him a full minute. She assimilated that he looked like the posters of seasoned army men. He looked rough, as if he could do whatever had to be done, wherever it was happening. She said, "I'll let you rest until supper's ready. Can you get up to eat? Or would you prefer a tray?"

He was sorely tempted. If he couldn't leave the bed, she wouldn't have the heart to oust him. But he couldn't be that much trouble. "Do you have a robe?"

She smiled just a little wickedly and suggested, "Pink lace?"

My God, he thought, I have to see her in that. He said soberly, "It wouldn't go with my eyes."

She laughed again and left the room.

He called, "Be sure to cancel the doc coming around."

Her voice was so nice. "Okay."

He lay there like a spoiled, ratty dog and smiled at his world. He sighed and coughed a little, calling his attention to the idle cigarette. He eased up, opened the window and put the cigarette into his mouth, lighted it and inhaled.

Since the cigarette was now on the endangered list, he savored the smoke, holding it in his lungs and then blew it slowly out of the window, being careful none of it touched the crisp, clean white ruffled curtains.

When the cigarette had burned down to a nub, he took the butt and the ashes in his hand and sneaked into the bathroom to flush it away. Then he carefully washed his hands and face, thinking that would wipe away all trace. With their impaired sense of smell, smokers always thought that way.

As he went back to his room, he peeked into the kitchen and saw Sara holding her head. She was distressed? Was his being there giving the staid woman problems? He couldn't allow that. Gently he asked, "Are you okay? What's the matter?"

"Nothing." She assured him. "It's just the crooked hair roots."

Standing there in just his undershorts, he researched that idea and found no reference in his mental files. "You have dishonest hair?"

"No. I have a headache."

He frowned. She was distressed that he was in her house? He asked, "Tension?"

"No. I changed my part and the hair roots object. They're hurting."

"Aw. Nasty roots." Didn't she notice that he was almost naked? "Want me to rub them for you?"

"They won't even allow that."

"You could sit on my lap while I rock you and sing to them?"

She blushed as she laughed. "Thanks, anyway." Then she had to inquire, "What sort of singer are you?"

"Brilliant."

"Of course."

While she'd said the right words, he didn't think she sounded sincere. He chose his words with some care. "Where I grew up, we were in plays and musicals all our young lives. We had no choice."

"In a 'home'?"

"Yeah." That was true, the Browns had made the house into a home where their real and diverse children had grown up.

"I didn't know children were still raised in orphanages. Weren't you ever in a foster home?"

"For a time. But the home where I lived was perfect."

"I'm glad. You must have made the transition to the army very well. Being used to being in a group, that way."

"Yeah." He'd never known he could be so crafty. It was a challenge and he was enjoying it. Or... He felt a tiny squirm inside his conscience.... Maybe she was just naive. Or honest. She probably was one of those who was honest and assumed everyone else was, too. "Did you cancel the doctor?" He was calling her attention to his body.

"You have an appointment at ten tomorrow. His nurse said she could come over any time. She saw you on a TV blurb about the six o'clock news. I said you didn't need her."

"What's she look like?"

Sara became indignant and covered it quite nicely, but she made his ego lift.

She asked, "What does one feed a mouse?"

"Do you have any birdseed with that bird cage?"

"Actually, I do feed the birds. Will mice eat birdseed?"

"Let's try it."

Sara went to the kitchen and got a small saucer which she filled with some birdseed from the sack. She came back into the living room, and they went over to the bird cage.

Mike took the little saucer and opened the cage door, setting the container on the floor of the cage by the little bowl of water already there.

The mouse was a real nothing. It had no ambition to live in a bird cage and eat bird food, and it didn't try to be charming or cute. A zero.

Sara suggested again, "How about driving out into the country and leaving it by a fence line?"

He needed the mouse until he was established in her house. "We'll have to make a few more honest tries before I solve the mouse."

"Flush?" She looked troubled.

"Or something."

"It isn't a pet. It doesn't try to be friendly. It's lazy and dumb. We ought to let it go back to nature."

Mike wondered if he should be more charming so that she didn't put him out in the field. "I wonder where Teddy caught him."

"I'll ask tomorrow. The mouse ought to be back with his family."

"How do you know he's a him?"

"No decent female would be a mouse."

Mike loved that. "There have to be some," Mike considered. "If there weren't, there wouldn't be any little mice."

"True. Teddy's is probably a pregnant female and we'll be inundated with mice, just like Australia."

He mostly noticed that she had again included him in the fate of the mouse. This time it was being inundated with them, so he'd have to be there to share that experience. Or did she just mean the town of Byford? He answered readily enough: "I think Australia's gotten their mouse problem under control. That was a couple of years ago."

She guessed, "The Australians threw the mice into the ocean, and they swam clear over here?"

He appeared to consider that and replied slowly, "I'd doubt that."

She grinned at him. Then she really looked at him and saw that he wasn't suitably dressed to be running around in her living room. She said, "Uh..."

And he watched as her eyes took him in, in darting glances, and she licked her lips. He had to breathe through his mouth, but he didn't move as he watched her blush.

Why did all the women in Byford blush? The hotel clerk, the waitress and Sara Benton all blushed. And he liked it. He liked her face and her blush and her body and her jiggle and her humor and her jealousy for him.

If he handled everything just right, she would be in his bed with him that night. Maybe not. She thought he was too badly injured. He was trapped in his own subterfuge, because he couldn't seem too healthy or she might let him sleep in his car.

He'd have to appear fragile for another day or two. Then he could recover... sufficiently.

She said, "Thank you for putting the birdseed in the cage with the mouse. I couldn't have done that."

"You'd have taken him out into the countryside?"

"I don't know what I would have done. I suppose I would have found a way to sneak him into your car." She lifted her eyebrows and said sassily, "You're traveling alone, and he could be company for you."

"You're all heart." He said that insincerely, squinting his eyes in a mean way.

She laughed.

He turned carefully and started back to—his—room. She went into the kitchen, apparently accepting that he would be there and that he could go into that room just as if he were staying there. He gave a sigh, as if he'd made it to a goal, and he got back into bed.

He relished the clean cotton sheets and the comfort of a double bed. It wasn't as big as the hotel bed, but it was adequate for a man alone. He was very comfortable. He listened to the sounds she made in the kitchen, fixing him a meal. He was contented. He hadn't felt that for a long time.

Well, he wasn't entirely contented, but even anticipation was a part of his feeling of well-being. There was the fact that she was there, she'd accepted that he would be also. That led to all sorts of anticipations.

But not tonight. It would be too soon for her. Probably.

He didn't dare to drowse, he would be awake all night with her right in the next room in that silent little house. He wouldn't be able to get up or pace or smoke or anything. He needed to stay awake. He yawned and stretched with considerable care.

She wakened him with great reluctance. "Mike? Your steak is just perfect. You need to eat it now, then you can go back to sleep."

So. Maybe his body knew what it was doing? With his wakening, she had just agreed that he should go back to sleep after he'd eaten? Here. In this bed.

She said, "I hated to waken you, but—"

And he smiled at her.

His hair was still army-short, but his sun-bleached eyebrows were unruly and his lashes were thick. His face wounds made him look look like a pirate. And his blue eyes were lazy and sleepy.

She wanted to put her hands on him. She wanted to lay his head against her and soothe him. She wanted to— She needed to feed him. "Can you come to the table?"

"Sure."

She saw how carefully he moved, and she said, "Let me get you a tray." She turned and started away.

"No. Really. It's better for me to move around and get used to it."

She stood and witnessed him get out of bed, still in just his shorts. She got his shirt from the closet and helped him into it. "Are your feet warm?" She squatted down to feel them. "You should have on socks. Sit down. I'll get them for you."

He sat down and watched her busyness as she fetched the socks, then she knelt down and worked them onto his feet. He loved her attention. No one had ever cared for him before in all his life . . . that he remembered. No one had ever put socks on him. He felt such a tenderness for her.

She reminded him, "You'll want to wash."

So he went into the bathroom. He was a little awkward about relieving himself, but she'd handled giving him the opportunity the whole day long. She was used to considering children's needs, and she was simply carrying that through to him. Did she consider him just another responsibility?

Well, she had blushed. That remembrance gave him a little heart. She knew he was a male. A grown male. Verified. He washed his hands and acknowledged himself in the mirror. He ran a wet hand over his hair and it lay tamed. It was the only thing on him that was.

He went out of the bathroom, down the short hallway and over to the dining room. She was busily putting his meal on the table.

She had contrived a pretty table, and a place had been set for just him. "Aren't you eating?"

"I've eaten." She looked at her watch. "It's time for the local news. You'll be on it. I've set the VCR so we can record it. Would you like to watch it here? This little TV is just black-and-white."

"Sure."

So she turned it on. He could hear the other TV in the living room as an echo to the one on the table. The screen was about five inches wide, but the picture was very sharp.

He looked at his plate and saw the perfect steak. It was crusty and steaming hot. He cut a piece and the meat bled. He smiled up at Sara.

She said, "Ugh."

And he laughed.

Then he noted the baked potato had been split for a swirl of sour cream with cut chives sprinkled over that. The salad was just right. There were slivered carrots and green beans, and on the little plate by his fork were two hot hard rolls. And his wineglass was a larger one of red wine. He'd never seen such a perfect dinner. Of course, he had. He glanced up to smile at Sara. No. No meal had ever been like this one. He ate the first bite. Ahhh. Perfect.

The national news was first. But after the commercials, the announcer said, "Today we had a hero from the Persian Gulf visit the Stephen Decatur Elementary School—"

And Mike put down his fork to say, "Good God."

Sara laughed and said, "You were a hero, remember? When we were late getting back, you got us by Mrs. Atwood."

He went back to eating, but he did glance over at the TV and he saw that Sara watched avidly. When his television image took off his shirt to show his wounds, Mike was watching her face, which sobered, and she frowned a little to see the damage to him again.

His conscience did twinge, as he allowed her to think it had been that bad. It hadn't. After he'd found out the pelting fusillade hadn't castrated him, nothing was that bad. But he couldn't reassure her until he was established in her house.

The phone began to ring.

People were looking for Mike. "Where is he?"

"Well, he's...here."

"May we come by? Herbert has talked of nothing else."

"Well, let me check. He isn't very strong yet, and this was a tiring day." She put the phone against her nice chest and said to Mike, "It's Herbert's parents. They would like to see you. Would a brief visit be all right?"

He turned out a hand and shrugged. "Sure."

"How soon."

He looked at his plate and the wine left. "An hour?"

She consulted her watch. "You probably ought to be in bed by then."

He could agree to that. He said nothing and just chewed with relishing little sounds in his throat.

She found that erotic.

He suggested, "A half hour?"

She gave that information to Herbert's parents and cautioned, "He isn't yet very strong. You should stay only briefly."

That was the first call.

Then the mayor called. "We thought a town meeting would be nice. A celebration that it's over and the guys are starting to come home."

"And the women—" She was a stickler and added that to his sentence.

"Yeah. And the gals. Can Mike do it?"

"I'll ask."

"Do you know where he's staying?"

"Well." She couldn't say he was indigent. "He's here."

"With you?"

"Yes."

"Oh."

Rather persimmonously she stated, "There are adequate facilities."

"Oh, yes! Sure! Right!" There was a pregnant pause, and the mayor said, "We'll be in touch."

As she put the phone down, Mike inquired, "You sounded p-p-pipped. Some problem?"

"They seem to question whether you should be staying with me."

He saw the light of battle in her eyes and her tightened lips. She was an obstinate woman. Now she would keep him there out of perversity? Hallelujah! "Need any backup? I can kill almost anything any number of ways."

She looked down her nose at her guest. "I can handle it."

He loved it.

And Timothy Pearson came by. He wasn't at all what Mike had expected. He was large and formidable. He didn't look anything like a teacher. He looked like a special-services infiltrator and killer, for God's sake. And he knew...wines? Maybe he had a high voice.

But Tim smiled just the faintest little bitty–bit and asked Mike in a rich bass voice deliberately lightened, "Staying?"

Mike looked him right in the eye and said, "Yeah."

And Tim said, "Miss Benton asked that I bring you a robe. I hope it isn't too large."

"I can handle it."

Sara contributed, "Byford is going to have a town meeting for Mike. Isn't that wonderful?"

"Wonderful." But Tim wasn't really agreeing, he was tasting the word to see if it fit. His tone made that doubtful.

Mike got up from the table to take the robe from Tim. Then he went into "his" room to change. He did that to show Tim he was wearing only a shirt and his drawers. Also he wanted to put on the robe by himself, in case the sleeves went down over his hands.

They did not.

That comforted Mike unreasonably. He then stood straight and tied the cord around his body with some flair. So. He was human. He wanted to look good to Sara. He smoothed his hair. Scratched his beard and decided to leave it, and he returned to the dining room where he interrupted an almost quarrel between Tim and Sara.

With some fire and deadly serious, Sara was finishing a sentence, '—here.'

"I believe it would be better if he—"

And she repeated, "Here."

Tim then reluctantly turned to Mike and said, "You could stay with me."

"That's kind of you," Mike replied. "I've already slept in the bed." Mike paused to allow Tim to assimilate that, then he continued kindly, "No sense in messing up two of them. Would you like a mouse? We're having problems finding it a home." He had used the term "we" with only a slight emphasis.

Tim narrowed his eyes.

Sara explained the mouse, ending up with, "So we had to bring it home."

She'd included Mike in the ownership or responsibility of the mouse.

Tim looked at Mike with real distaste.

Mike smiled like a friend. He sat down and finished his meal, sipping the wine. He looked at it against the light and rolled it on his tongue with thoughtful doubt. He was tampering with Tim's limits.

He could do that. He was an injured warrior, home from foreign lands. And he had Sara on his side. Not only was he her guest, but she was a woman who harbored a mouse that revolted her.

Hmmm. Maybe *he* revolted her and she just cared for him because he'd written the kids back? He scowled and glared at the wine.

Tim inquired, "Not to your palate?"

Mike lifted gently inquiring eyebrows.

Tim underlined it. "The wine."

Mike picked it up. "A nice frivolous little wine. Did you have some?"

Tim put his tongue hard on his bottom lip, then replaced it with his teeth to prevent himself from speaking right away.

Sara supplied, "Tim chose that wine." She tilted her head a little and enquired, "Don't you like it?"

"I would have guessed Tim had chosen it." He smiled and set his half-filled glass down with a finality.

Sara wasn't stupid. She could feel the odd tension. She was a teacher. If this were the school playground and hostilities threatened, which one would she sent to Mrs. Atwood? Mike. He was the instigator. Instead of being annoyed with him for taunting Tim, he amused her in an impatient way. Males were so predictable.

Herbert's parents arrived. Herbert wasn't with them. That surprised Sara. They came in with their stares riveted on Mike, as if approaching a guru. They said, "Herbert came home and talked to us." They said, "He's always treated adults as if they weren't too bright and wouldn't understand anything he said." They said, "He came home and told us that you said war was stupid." They explained, "Herbert had said that all along. We had tried to explain to him why we were in the Persian Gulf."

Mike just looked at them.

That didn't bother them at all. They were in some shock. They had to share it with Mike.

He appeared to understand and allowed them to babble on about the change in Herbert, so that they could clear out their amazement and begin to function. They *had* to talk about it.

Mike said, "You never let kids realize you think they're too smart." That was a Salty rule. "You always compliment them for any victory, and then give them something baffling to handle, like a recalcitrant dog or a motor. He's not too young to start learning about motors.''

With awe, Herbert's parents accepted those pearls from Mike's lips.

Sara's friend, Marilyn, came over. She had called. She hadn't mentioned coming over. She had black hair, dancing green eyes and a great smile. She was a nice height. Her figure was excellent. So was her sense of humor.

Sara took several deep breaths and looked at the ceiling as she pinched her mouth together.

Tim was silent. He moved and breathed like a man who was containing himself with great discipline.

Herbert's parents continued to babble, Marilyn listened attentively and Mike absently drank the rest of his glass of wine, savoring it.

Tim could only grind his teeth. He couldn't call attention to Mike having drunk the wine. To do so would be too adolescent.

Mike set the empty glass on the table and was aware that it had been a treat. He glanced up and saw the disgruntled Tim, who knew that Mike had relished the wine. Mike grinned to share the humor.

Tim was not amused.

Mike leaned back and sighed in great contentment. He ran fingers into a nonexistent shirt pocket, then tapped the pockets of the robe. No cigarettes. He started to rise to go get them and remembered he could not smoke in Her house.

Mike looked at her sitting there, patiently allowing Herbert's parents to release all the words they needed to expend. Then he glanced at Tim, who was watching him with grisly humor. He knew Mike wanted a cigarette.

And shrewdly, Mike wondered if Tim had smoked...and quit for Sara? He looked back at Sara. Any man would quit for her.

Of course, right now she was approaching the peak of her physical perfection. She was not a child or an uncertain or too self-conscious young woman. She was mature and confident.

She was probably a shrew. She was obstinate and determined. She'd become a harridan. A man would get tangled in her web and she'd kill him just like the black widow spider.

Had she been Tim's lover? Was she?

Mike found that idea disturbed him too much.

That he would feel so possessive of this obstinate woman, having known her less than twelve hours, was probably only because she was the first woman who'd zonked him since he'd found out he was mortal, after all, and still capable.

Mike looked at a fellow man and enquired of Tim, "When did you quit?"

"Last October 10."

Mike nodded in empathy. Tim could probably even relate the time and circumstances. That Tim had blurted the exact date and bitten his lip to punish it, showed that he still suffered withdrawal.

Marilyn volunteered the information, "I never started smoking. So I don't know what it would be like to quit."

Neither Mike nor Tim responded with even a glance.

Mike looked over at Sara. Giving up smoking was an irritating chore. Would she be worth it? He'd have to be sure.

Five

It was as Herbert's parents were apologizing for taking up so much time, that the idea came and sat on Mike's shoulder. "Instead of a recalcitrant dog," he suggested thoughtfully, "why not a neat, silent mouse? We have one you could take home this very night."

"A mouse?" Herbert's mother questioned that with serious hesitation.

Uh-oh. Mike said soothingly, "It won't bark and bother the neighbors, and it won't mess up your yard. The mouse can be taught all sorts of tricks. Herbert can build interesting mazes for it to try to solve."

Herbert's father exclaimed in wonder, "Of course!"

Admiringly Marilyn commented, "That's such a good idea." And her smile for Mike made Sara bristle.

Herbert's parents took the bird cage home with them, the mouse inside, and carried a sack with a respectable amount of birdseed.

During the entire transaction, Mike and Sara had not exchanged one glance.

Inside the house, nothing was said until the car had driven away. At last Mike allowed himself to look at Sara and they both laughed. Then Mike said, "Do you realize this will be the beginning of a friendship between Herbert and Teddy? The mouse will change Herbert's life."

And Sara said with great tenderness, "Not the mouse. You. You've touched all our lives."

Marilyn agreed.

Tim choked in such a way that Mike inquired solicitously, "Bone caught in your throat? Here, let me help." And he swatted Tim on the back and jarred even that big man.

Tim whipped his head around to see Mike's blandly concerned expression.

Then Mike had the gall to inquire, "Okay?"

Tim ground out through clenched teeth, "Not yet." And his look was murderous.

Sara asked, "Tim, could you drop Marilyn off on your way? I hate for her to walk home with it so dark."

Tim looked outside.

Even Mike saw that it was barely dusk.

Marilyn said, "I can walk."

So Tim had to say, "No, I'll drop you."

Marilyn grinned and said, "Not on my head, hear?"

Tim gave her a patient look. "Maybe you ought to stay here tonight. With Brown so—fragile—Sara might need help."

"Okay."

"That's not necessary." Sara was a little strident.

But *Mike* agreed! "It might be a good idea." He knew he would have to stay out of Sara's bed that one night, anyway, so he might just as well appear harmless to Sara.

That stumped Tim, who brightened—but it annoyed Sara, who frowned at Mike in some temper.

Marilyn said, "I'll just hop over to the house and get a nightgown."

"No!" Sara rose and stood staunchly. "I do not need any 'help' or company or someone else in the house. I don't want to share my bed. Mike has the other room, and the sofa is too small. There isn't accommodation for anyone else. Thank you, Marilyn, but you do understand." It was not a question.

Marilyn grinned and said, "Darn."

Tim began, "Now, Sara—"

But Sara interrupted. "Will you drop Marilyn off on your way? Today has been long enough for a man in Mike's condition."

On cue, Mike wilted a little.

A bit stridently, Tim said, "I don't like his being here."

Sara lifted her chin. "He's my guest."

Tim stood up. "You don't know him!"

In denial, Sara listed her knowledge of Mike. It was a short list. "We've corresponded all this time. He wrote to the kids. He's a good man." She even added: "He has no place else to go." She faced Tim down.

"Will you please take Marilyn home on your way?" Her voice was cool.

Tim recognized the fact that he could not win. There was no way he was going to interfere with Sara at this time. So he had to make do with a really hard look at Mike and say in a very serious manner, "You be careful."

Now, that could have meant Mike was to be careful of himself, but Tim's voice tone was wrong. He was threatening Mike with mayhem.

Was Mike threatened? No, he smiled just a little and his eyes lighted up. Tim had just proved that, like the wines, he knew women, so obviously Sara could be worth any effort.

Mike stood up and said to Tim, "Thank you for lending me your robe. That was nice of you." The words were just right, but the sound of one-upmanship was laced through them. And just looking at Tim's reaction to such gratitude, Mike knew Tim would never again wear that robe. If Mike gave it back, Tim would burn it. If he bought Tim a new robe, Tim would burn it, too. Somehow, Tim didn't appear to have any fondness for Mike.

So Mike went over and stood by Sara, as if he was half of the hosts, being patient about waiting for their guests to leave.

That just about did it for Tim, but there wasn't any way, at all, that he could frog-jump Mike out of Sara's house. If Tim left quietly, then he could return to Sara's house another time. He couldn't jeopardize the scant foothold he'd managed with Sara by quarreling with Mike, or trying to oust him or trying to reason with Sara that Mike was a fox in the chicken house. Tim said to Marilyn, "Let's go."

Sara allowed them to leave without saying goodbye to them. She closed the door and took a deep breath. "People are strange."

She said that. She did. Mike smiled a little. "They were fairly normal. You should see some of the guys in the army. It would make you shiver to think they're our first line."

"You're normal. No, you're not—"

He went still.

"—you're superior."

Now, how was he supposed to argue with that? "I'm just a guy." He smiled his sweetest smile. He was so amused.

"Would you like a drink? I suppose you're dying for a cigarette. I saw you blowing smoke out the back window. I thought for a minute the house was on fire."

"Caught me, did you?"

"You simply can't sneak around, trying to outfox a teacher. We know all the tricks."

And he smiled like a Cheshire cat. "When did you quit smoking?"

"Long ago, in my misspent youth."

"How...misspent?" he asked hopefully.

"I went to Padre Island with a car full of females and we rented a condo."

"Glory be!"

"You can well be impressed. And I smoked."

"Well now, Sara, I am shocked."

"And I continued to smoke for several months. But I quit when I realized I was becoming addicted."

"Addicted!"

"I got up to smoking three a day."

He acted impressed.

"Three cigarettes," she clarified that.

"Rampant." He didn't smile.

"Yes. So you can see that I do understand your problem. But if you would even...if a woman...if you kissed someone, she would taste the smoke on your... mouth."

"Not my mouth."

"How would you get rid of the film it leaves on your...surfaces."

"I wash."

"But your hands are filmed and everywhere you touch, you would leave the odor of cigarettes."

"Smell me." His voice had gone almost as husky and raspy as his adoptive father's. His gaze was avid.

She didn't move or reply, and he was paralyzed, waiting to see what she would do. Would she...touch him?

She moved to him with all the speed of a glacier. He was riveted. She came so slowly to him that he was having trouble breathing as he waited to see what she would touch...what she...might...smell around. He'd become petrified.

She came nearer, watching his eyes. He was in thrall. She was closer. His lips parted and he panted shallow little gasps of air, almost silently. He couldn't blink.

He was taller than she, but he didn't lean over a little or bend his head down to make it easier for her. No. She would have to stretch up his body and she would have to touch her body against his. His entire front anticipated being touched.

She put one hand on his shoulder and stretched up to sniff along his mouth. His hair ends lifted out from

his head as if he'd put a finger in a socket. Other parts
of him reacted similarly.

She felt breathless. She pulled her head back and
looked at him very seriously. He was excited. His
breathing was irregular. His attention was rigidly
concentrated on her. She ought to back off. She
should.

She smelled along his chest. His chin touched down
just above her head as he watched her do that. His
breaths stirred her hair. His breathing was hot. So was
his body. He had a fever?

She looked up at him again and his eyes were
bloodshot! That was a sign of fever. She put her hand
on his forehead and felt it. It burned her hand. "Do
you have a fever?" She was alarmed.

"Yes."

"I'll call Dan back."

"Dan?"

"My doctor."

"Ladies don't call doctors by their first names."

"We were in kindergarten together."

"Oh."

"You are so hot."

"Yeah. Feel my stomach." He opened Tim's robe
and wondered if Tim had ever pulled this ploy on
Sara. Then Mike remembered he had no condoms.
Yes, he did. There were a couple in his war bag. It was
in the trunk of his car. He said, "I haven't been kissed
in a very long time. Is it still nice?"

So she had to kiss him. She lifted her soft mouth
and closed her eyes. He almost lost consciousness, but
he bravely lowered his mouth as his arms went around
her sweet body. He pulled her close . . . and kissed her.
It was mind-blowing. When he lifted his mouth, her

head wobbled, but his arms were wrapped around her very tightly so she didn't falter.

He kissed her again.

It was the Fourth of July? Already? And she realized when Cary Grant kissed Grace Kelly in *To Catch A Thief* the fireworks had been in *them,* not outside.

When he sucked in his breath as she moved, she realized she'd hurt something on him. She held still, but she stiffened. "I hurt you."

He agreed, "It does hurt."

"Oh, Mike, I'm so sorry." She released herself from his reluctant arms and talked the entire time. "I should have been more considerate. The smoking doesn't matter that much. Of course, if we'd kept the mouse, it could have acted as the canaries did in the bottom of mines. When the air got too bad the canaries stopped singing. They were dead. I could have periodically checked the mouse."

He replied, "I'll get you another."

"No!"

"Then how will you know if the air is polluted?"

"I'll be dead."

"I'll smoke out the window."

"I just hope the neighbors don't turn a hose on you."

"I did mention I need a shower."

"You smell marvelous."

Her voice sound and her words just about ruined his control.

She explained, "Men smell different."

"How many men have you been sniffing around?"

"Just one, so far."

"One's enough," he decided. "You don't need any more experience doing that."

"I could write a thesis!"

"No!"

"Why, how limiting you are!"

"It's been done." He dismissed further study. "*The National Geographic* conducted an extensive test on smells. The subscribers participated."

"In what?"

"Smells. Cloves, nutmeg, sweat, that sort of thing."

"I would limit myself to just men's bodies."

"You'd be mobbed."

"By whom?" She was curious and listened for his reply.

"By MEN who want to be smelled by you!"

"Well, that's just silly. Just because you'd hold still for me to smell you, what man would stop what he was doing so that I could smell him?"

"You'd be very surprised. And you'd be even more surprised after you started sniffing around."

"Because they don't bathe?"

She appeared honestly curious. He couldn't believe her. She knew what had happened when she'd smelled around on him. Was she dense? "It's erotic."

"What's...erotic?"

"For a woman to smell around like that on a man. For you to do that to me."

"Did I offend you?"

"Hell, no!"

"Then why are you complaining?"

Frustrated, he exploded. "I'm NOT! God! What a stupid woman you are."

"I have my Master's." She was indignantly defensive.

He was stridently positive, "It wasn't in *men*."

"Of course not! I know very little about men. If I did, I wouldn't have to smell around on you."

He yelled, "I like you doing that!"

"Then why are you yelling at me?"

"Because you set me on my ear. Don't you realize that?"

"You're back to being angry with me, and you just said you weren't."

"You turn me on." He said the words through his teeth.

She looked startled, then she smiled a little. "Really?"

"Yeesss!"

"Well, how amazing! I don't believe I've ever managed to do that before. It must be because you've been gone from the States so long."

He swung away so his back was to her and he said to the ceiling, "Good God Almighty. Give me strength."

"Why?"

He turned back to her. "Are you actually, really and truly, honestly that dumb?"

She frowned a little and asked, "About...what?"

And he yelled in his field voice, "MEN!"

"I've dated." She was snippy.

He was leaning over at the waist and snarled, "Have you ever slept with a man?"

She snapped, "That isn't any of your business!"

He paced a way and lifted his arms up with the fists clenched and said, "God help me."

"Why?"

He turned and nailed her with a look. Just with a LOOK, he did that. He said to her, "You are not God."

"I am aware of that, I'm a woman."

"And I'm very aware of that."

"You don't like women?" That apparently hadn't occurred to her before then.

"Yes."

"Then why are you in such a snit? I kissed you and you've been furious ever since."

"I want you."

She waited as he glowered at her. She encouraged, "To do...what?"

"Don't you know anything?"

"Why are you so angry?"

"Sara. How old are you?"

"Thirty-five."

"Are you trying to tell me that you have never, before now, realized that you're a very sexy woman and that you have had Tim in the palm of your hand for over six months?"

"Tim? I haven't paid that much attention to him."

"You haven't?"

"No. We're friends."

"You haven't slept with him?"

"Good gracious, no."

"Why not?"

"I don't want to."

"Then you ought not let him hang around."

"I don't encourage him."

"Apparently he hasn't given up hope. He thinks of you as his."

"Don't be silly."

"Of all the things in this whole world on which you can rely, you have to know that I know men."

"Hooray for you."

"How could you possibly have gotten to be thirty-five years old and not realized men are very easily triggered?"

"They get mad?"

He was incredulous. "What do you read?"

"Read? Who has the time?" She sighed. "I mostly work on school papers. Or I make integrated thematic units for the class, or I go to seminars on teaching, or I attend parent/teacher conferences or try to get kids to try harder or to behave or to get along with each other. I read books and I watch programs that will help in some way."

"Don't you ever go out and have any fun?"

"Oh, yes."

"Doing...what?"

She gave him an aloof glance. "I have kissed other men besides you."

"Have you ever had a kiss flutter your...stomach?"

"How did you know that?"

"I read a different kind of book."

"Your kiss did that to my stomach. It makes me want another kiss, to see if it will happen again."

Mike groaned and clutched his hair.

"NOW why are you angry?"

He sighed as he dropped his hands down alongside his hips and he said in a disgruntled way, "I suppose now you'll tell me you're a virgin."

She tightened her mouth and looked aside, as if he'd offended her.

"So you're not?"

"It isn't any—"

"—of my business. I know. It really isn't. You couldn't have survived this long, sniffing around that way, and still be... untouched. I think that's the word."

"The word for... what?"

"For a woman who hasn't been with a man."

She huffed a couple of times.

He said, "Oh, go to bed."

Rather snootily, she told him, "I have to clean up the kitchen."

"I'll help."

"No."

He looked at her. "Who would have believed I'd get myself into this kind of mess?"

And right on target, she asked, "What... mess?" And she frowned at him.

"Just the fact that you don't know tells volumes."

"I've always wanted to use that expression about something speaking volumes. Have you managed it very often?"

"Yes. Just lately."

"At the war?"

"Here in Byford."

"You think I don't know much about men, don't you."

"Yes."

"Well, you will see you're wrong. I'm not as inexperienced as you believe. Just wait. You will see."

"How about now?"

"There isn't anyone else here."

"You need an audience?" He was surprised.

"I need a subject."

"I'll sacrifice myself."

"You're the observer."

"You want me to... watch?"

"How else can you be convinced?"

He was so stunned that he could think of no reply. "I don't believe this." He went out to his car and brought in his paraphernalia. He stood under the shower for a while, and the water loosened the bandages. He eased them off and threw them away.

He did get into bed, but he spent most of the night leaning out the window, blowing smoke out under the ruffles of the lifted priscilla curtains. He questioned why he would be brought up against such a peculiar woman. In this day and age, how could any woman be that isolated from living? Just television should have given her some clue. Didn't she watch the soaps? Some of those steamed the inside of the glass tube.

She couldn't have all her marbles. She wasn't working with a full deck. Sometime in her childhood, she must have been dropped on her head.

But having her sniff around on him, that way, had been the most erotic thing that had ever happened to him. Just to think of her doing that about had him cross-eyed. How could she do something that erotic and not be affected?

Well, she had been. She said it had made the inside of her stomach flutter, so that she wanted to do it again and see if her stomach would do it again.

She was treating him as a guinea pig? For him to respond so naturally, she had to know what she was doing. She apparently had no idea.

He blew out another cloud of smoke and tried to remember if he'd taken a drag on his cigarette or if that smoke was from his overheated libido. She was driving him wild.

As she undressed for bed, Sara contemplated the red garter belt holding up her stockings. Had they caused that eventful day? Was the garter belt the reason Mike was now in her spare room? She looked dreamily into the mirror, not even seeing her reflection. He was just on the other side of that wall.

She smiled a little mushily. He would be naked on the bed and restless. She'd seen that once in a movie. He would lie there, suffering because she wasn't with him. He would be yearning for her.

She looked somewhat smug. It was the garter belt. It was that which had made her so reckless. She'd wear it again the next day and she would just see what would happen.

She put on a large T-shirt and crawled into bed to stretch and turn a bit, but it had been a long day, and before she knew it, she was asleep.

He finally got to sleep and didn't waken until the telephone rang off the wall. It was that she-cat. She told him, "Your appointment with Dan is in just forty-five minutes. I left your breakfast on the kitchen table. Are you all right?"

"Yeah . . . for the circumstances."

"Do you hurt?"

"Like bloody hell."

"Oh, Mike. Do you really want to go to the town meeting on Saturday?"

"If I live that long."

"Oh, Mike."

"Honey, my wounds are fine. It's you sniffing around that's wrecked me."

"I did that? How could that possibly have affected you in such a way?"

"Come home and I'll show you."

She was silent. "Mike, are you all right?"

"Yeah."

"I don't always understand you."

"I'm a simple man."

"No."

"Yes. A simple man with simple needs."

There was a long silence. "Mike, have we been talking about sexual . . . attraction? Was that the real subject of our discussions last night?"

"Yes."

"Oh."

There was a longer silence, then she softly hung up.

Mike figured that tore it. There went the whole ball of wax.

He found cereal and fresh fruit on the kitchen table. The strawberries were like nothing he'd had in quite a while. The coffee was hot and excellent. He dressed and went to the address she'd left on the table for his appointment with Dan, her doctor.

In the doctor's office, spring colds and allergies were apparent. Mike's problems were a little different.

Dan was lanky and blond. It turned out that he was a CHAMPUS doctor. Mike was his first military patient under that order. Dan mentioned that. "We have to agree to treat the patient for the government's price. So that's why you have to lie on the hood of your car, this way, instead of the examination table inside."

On the examination table, Mike said, "Ha-ha-ha." Then, as Dan searched out the various intrusions to his tender body, Mike asked, "Can we have a doctor-patient confidential discourse?"

Dan replied, "I read in this morning's paper you're the houseguest of Sara Benton. How did you manage that?"

"By surprise. She said you've known her for some time. I need to know—is she as innocent as she seems? As unknowing?"

Dan stood up straight, so that he could look Mike in the eye. "I believe I'd consider giving up a leg to know your reason for those questions. But, yes, she is. She's quite literal, and completely unaware of herself. She's driven guys nuts since she was about ten. She's completely out in left field thinking about something else. Guys eventually just give up and find a woman who is a little more alert to life and to them."

"I honestly can't believe she's real."

"I wish I could give you some hope that you might be the one who makes the...uh...breakthrough, but you should hear some of the stories from the guys who've tried. Tim has been the most persistent. You must know that your being Sara's houseguest has his teeth pointed and his knuckles dragging the ground. He's a tad jealous."

"He has no reason. She doesn't understand men or their ramifications at all. She set me on my ear last night and *she* thought I'd been offended!"

"Yeah," Dan agreed. "That sounds just like her. I'll get some of the guys together and we'll all have some beer and laugh at ourselves for being so stupid. We won't ask Tim. Like these war wounds of yours, his scars are still too new."

"But she's thirty-five!"

"With a difference in the numbers, guys have been saying something like that, just that way, for some time now. We figure she'll die an old maid and still be a virgin."

"She is?"

"Yeah."

Hostile, Mike frowned harshly at Dan.

"Listen, I'm not giving anything away. Everyone knows that. It's common knowledge. If any guy had ever convinced her, he wouldn't have said a word. Each guys tells how clever he was in trying for her, and then he tells her misunderstanding. It's always hilarious... after a couple of years. She's impossible."

Then Dan added, "But you're not." He indicated Mike's body. "You're going to be fine. It looks like you stood up and took the brunt of it. Are you that foolhardy?"

"I must be, if I'm going back to Sara's."

Dan patted the shoulder that was unsliced. "Have courage. No one else has ever been allowed to stay in her house."

"She thinks I'm an indigent orphan."

Dan sat down with a thump. "What a dodge! How'd you think of that? Brilliant!"

"She guessed it, and I didn't correct her."

"By George, you might be a match for her!"

"Believe me, I'm not. I yelled at her last night. I yelled at her and God."

"He understands. Other men have yelled at Him about her. Good luck. If it's at all possible, keep me informed. I'll root for you."

"What about Tim?"

"He's used up his chance."

"I don't believe he understands that."

"Given a few more days of you living there, and Tim'll give up. Marilyn would be just about right for Tim."

"Now, how do you know he took her home last night?"

"He did?"

"They were there, and Tim wanted Marilyn to stay with us."

"That's understandable."

"Sara refused, and insisted Tim take Marilyn home."

"Come again tomorrow—no charge, just keep me informed."

"Now, Daniel . . ."

"Only my mother says my name that way."

"I can understand her. I suppose you went into medicine so you could see people's insides?"

"Why else? I really wanted to open up heads," he confided candidly. "However, that takes more study. But I've always wanted to change brain convolutions and tidy people's thinking."

"I thought that was done with sound."

"You've been around the younger generation."

"Yeah."

"Promise you'll come in tomorrow. I don't tell a soul anything. But I'll go crazy until I know what's going on with you two."

"I'll see."

Dan cautioned: "Don't slit your wrists."

"Has someone done that over her?"

"Close."

Mike frowned. "My God, she's a hazard."

"I've been telling you that!"

"I'll see what I can do."

"Now, that's noble."

Six

_____

Dr. Dan Hobart parted with his new patient by saying, "Keep in touch. Preferably tomorrow at ten."

Mike frowned.

"Remember? I'm to be kept posted."

"How can a man be that curious?"

"I'm not stra— Oh, you mean inquisitive. You've never heard of hospital gossip?" Dan had to pause as he contemplated that possibility. "Gossip is rampant," he explained. "It becomes addictive," he elaborated. "We beat the old adage of over-the-back-fence gossip all hollow. And almost right away, we begin to get blasé with basic smug and need more shocking things to discu— Of course, I would _never_ betray a confidence and anything you tell me is sacrosanct. Trust me."

Mike eyed Dan in a very jaundiced manner. "You've never heard of army rumors?"

NO COST! NO OBLIGATION TO BUY! NO PURCHASE NECESSARY!

PLAY "LUCKY 7"
AND GET AS MANY AS SIX FREE GIFTS...

HOW TO PLAY:

1. With a coin, carefully scratch off the silver box at the right. This makes you eligible to receive two or more free books, and possibly other gifts, depending on what is revealed beneath the scratch-off area.

2. You'll receive brand-new Silhouette Desire® novels. When you return this card, we'll send you the books and gifts you qualify for *absolutely free*!

3. If we don't hear from you, every month, we'll send you 6 additional novels to read and enjoy. You can return them and owe nothing but if you decide to keep them, you'll pay only $2.49* per book, a saving of 40¢ each off the cover price. There is **no** extra charge for postage and handling. There are **no** hidden extras.

4. When you join the Silhouette Reader Service™, you'll get our subscribers'-only newsletter, as well as additional free gifts from time to time just for being a subscriber.

5. You must be completely satisfied. You may cancel at any time simply by sending us a note or a shipping statement marked ''cancel'' or by returning any shipment to us at our cost.

This lovely heart-shaped box is richly detailed with cut-glass decorations, perfect for holding a precious memento or keepsake—and it's yours absolutely free when you accept our no-risk offer.

PLAY "LUCKY 7"

**Just scratch off the silver box with a coin.
Then check below to see which gifts you get.**

YES! I have scratched off the silver box. Please send me all the gifts for which I qualify. I understand I am under no obligation to purchase any books, as explained on the opposite page.

225 CIS AGM4
(U-SIL-D-10/92)

NAME

ADDRESS   APT

CITY   STATE   ZIP

7	7	7	WORTH FOUR FREE BOOKS, FREE HEART-SHAPED CURIO BOX AND MYSTERY BONUS
🍒	🍒	🍒	WORTH FOUR FREE BOOKS AND MYSTERY BONUS
●	●	●	WORTH THREE FREE BOOKS
🔔	🔔	🍒	WORTH TWO FREE BOOKS

SILHOUETTE "NO RISK" GUARANTEE

If offer card is missing, write to: Silhouette Reader Service, 3010 Walden Ave., P.O. Box 1867, Buffalo, NY 14269-1867

"No! Really?"

"They probably aren't as anatomically correct as hospital gossip."

"True." Dan considered. "That's probably right. Still, I'm avidly interested in what happens between you and Sara. And if I can be of any help, don't hesitate to ask."

"How could you help?"

"I could distract Tim."

"How . . . would you distract Tim?"

Dan laughed. "I could find a new fishing hole—he's a fishing devotee—or I could dangle a blonde nurse in front of his eyes. We have a— Well, you wouldn't be interested right now."

Mike agreed and said goodbye. He promised to return the next day, if it was at all possible, and he left, walking out to his car.

He sat for a minute before inserting the key, and recognized that he felt gloomy. If in such a brief encounter, Dan knew he was zonked by Sara, he must have a bad case of her. In this short of time? It was impossible. Wasn't it?

He considered that he was still adjusting to being a temporary civilian. When his convalescent time was completed and he got back on base, he'd be fine.

The thought of leaving Sara alone in Byford, with Tim and his pointed teeth and dragging knuckles, didn't lift Mike's spirits at all.

He drove over to the school and sat looking at Sara's car. He remembered that it hadn't caught right when she'd started it after school the day before. And an idea formed.

He went inside the building and was greeted with great friendly smiles. His "hero" facade was still intact. He took advantage. "I need to switch cars with Sara," he confided to the secretary. "Is it okay if I see her to get her car keys?"

"Sure. Go ahead. You know which room."

He gave her one of his best smiles. "Thanks."

A thirty-six-year-old man knew how to handle women. He walked down the empty hall, with his stride making a male sound of power. Soldiers especially knew how to do that. He went to her room and just opened the door.

He surprised her. He surprised the kids, too, but it was Sara's surprise that riveted him. She looked up to frown, but when she saw him, her smile was like the benevolent sun.

He gave her his best smile. He wasn't aware of doing that one. He was just glad to see that she was real.

Then he realized the kids were being cheerfully noisy in greeting him. He lifted an index finger to his lips, and they hushed instantly, grinning. He looked them all over, saying, "Hello, John Two, Melissa, George, Herbert, Teddy, Susan, Peggy—" And, again, he named them all. He said, "I must speak to Miss Benton. Behave."

He took Miss Benton's arm and tugged her out into the hall. And he closed the door on smothered giggles. He glanced up and down the hall's briefly empty expanse, as he said, "I am your guest and you didn't kiss me good-morning." Giving her no time to speak her feeble excuse, he put his arms around her in a boa constrictor embrace and he kissed her to allow her to make up for that oversight.

When he lifted his mouth from his squishy kiss, there was a hair-lifting, skin-prickling sound of their parting mouths. Her pupils were enormous in those brilliantly blue eyes and she seemed boneless.

He propped her against the wall while he stood restlessly patient. Someone came out of a room down the hall and went on beyond out of sight.

He told her, "I came to switch cars with you. I need to get some work done on yours, because it didn't catch right yesterday when you led me to your den."

"House," she corrected, moving her mouth with some difficulty. Her glazed gaze was stuck on his face.

"A den of inequity," he agreed, as he glanced both ways down the hall. It was again clear, so he kissed her.

She wobbled after that one. He had to stand her on her feet and hold her arms before she recovered her equilibrium.

Maybe her seduction didn't need any coaxing or conversation or verbal acknowledgment. She was ready. He sure was. And he would still be in her house for a while, because her car would be in her garage with its guts strewn around and she'd have to be driving his car. He smiled into her brilliant blue eyes, like a cat who has caught a mouse.

He asked, "How's Herbert getting along with the mouse?"

She had to blink a time or two to realign her thinking and she replied, "Umph."

"Good." He smiled his cat smile.

As she struggled for coherence, one of the teachers exited a room and came down the hall. She spoke in a friendly manner, and Mike smiled at her.

Sara managed to say, "You were right... about Teddy and what's his name? Herbert. Yes. They talk. Herbert is becoming normaler... more normal."

To impart such wisdom, his voice became grave, "You must always listen to me. I am older and wiser. I am always right."

Her reaction to that statement only proved she was a shambles, because she nodded seriously.

His smile turned wolfish. And he kissed her a third and devastating time. Even he was shattered. He trembled so that his hair shook with the shimmers of need that shivered through all his nerve cells.

His eyes hot, he said to the mass of inertness that was Sara, "Get me your car keys."

And she obeyed like a hypnotized slave.

He stood in the hall, waiting, his hands in his trouser pockets, his shoulders hunched, his body urging action. He'd known her just over twenty-four hours.

In the army's debriefing of the returnees, they'd all been warned about this very thing. He needed to back off, cool down and give her some room.

Yes.

How about the other half of his bed? That ought to be room enough for her to—

She returned to the hall and solemnly held out the keys on her open palm. Soberly, she watched his fingers lift them from her hand, replacing them with his own car keys. Her cheeks were pink, her eyes earnest, her hair a little free.

He smiled.

Her lips parted.

To hell with the cautionings. He kissed her again.

Then he set her back from him, patted her bottom and turned to walk down the hall. He looked back at the corner, and she was still there, watching after him. He was enormously pleased. He lifted his hand in farewell and disappeared from her sight.

He drove back to her house and began to disembowel her car. Salty would have been proud of him.

It took most of the rest of that day.

When he had lunch, he had rummaged through her refrigerator and freezer and was astounded by the junk she preserved. He went to the store and got red meat and potatoes and real cheese and real cream.

He made a man's stew. There was enough for a battalion.

So when Sara came home, there were several... surprises for her. As she exited his blue automobile, she saw the strewn viscera with the dead-body shell of her own car. She gasped and put her hand to her heart. She faltered and her voice was unsteady. "Will you be able to...put it all back?"

He was indolent. "It might take a while." He lit a cigarette and inhaled in deep, slow, eye-slitting relish.

Having just witnessed one disaster, she did note his addicted pleasure. Her tongue said, "You'll never quit."

"This is my last one." He looked at her clear-eyed and serious.

She believed him.

But then, still in shock, she went into the house, and in the kitchen she saw the humongous church pot that had been a family heirloom. It was setting on two burners of the stove and it was holding something that smelled marvelous.

She cautiously approached the pot and gingerly lifted the heavy lid. It was true; it was chock full. She turned and inquired, "Who all are you intending to feed?"

While Sara was on the phone with dinner invitations, Mike busily opened out the table and helped set it. Then he went next door to introduce himself as Sara's houseguest. Oddly, they knew all about him. Their eyes were lively, as they willingly gathered the extra plates and encouraged him to expand on anything he'd like to say.

Back at Sara's house, Mike mentioned to her, "Your neighbors are very friendly."

She stopped dead in buckling her belt and asked, "Which neighbors—"

"Collins, isn't it?"

"You went over there?"

"We didn't have enough plates."

"Mike, I have boxes of plates in the basement. What did you say to them?"

"That we're having a dinner party."

"They are gossips." She turned her head and looked soberly out the window. She tilted her head a little in several directions. She moved her lips and she bit her lower lip. She took several quick breaths and she almost gestured a couple of times. But she controlled her need to censure him.

He watched her with a little smile on his face. He had her. Her car was undrivable, her friends were coming for dinner and the neighbors now all knew that he was in her house. But how could she evict a wounded war hero?

Tim was one of their guests. Mike had gently suggested Sara invite him and ask that Tim pick up Marilyn on his way there. Tim had done that. And Dan Hobart and his wife were there.

As they were sipping some of the wine Tim had donated, Mike said quietly, just to Dan, "This eliminates the appointment for ten tomorrow morning. You can see for yourself."

Dan watched his feet take a step and he advised, "When Sara called me, and I knew you were still at her house, I called your captain at your base down in Texas and checked you out. Sara is a lifelong friend."

"Did Phil clear me okay?"

"He said you're a good man—and he was very, *very* interested."

Mike laughed. "He would be."

And the men went out and viewed the incredible demolition of Sara's car.

Dan was especially impressed. "How did you ever think of doing that?"

Mike shrugged modestly and lit another "final" cigarette.

"Brilliant. And a joint-host party! You are really a maneuverer. They teach this kind of thing in the army?"

"Basic training." With a single nod, Mike moved a hand out to diminish the talent offhandedly.

Tim, being knowledgeable, understood just how long it would take to reassemble that car and he snapped the stem of his wineglass.

Dan did the bandaging on Tim's hand. Sara tried to fit the crystal stem back together. Tim—and Mike—saw that. She was more interested in the wineglass than in Tim's delicate flesh.

So Mike didn't have to worry about Sara being entrapped by Tim, he needed only to convince Tim to back off. He was working on it.

At the dinner table, Mike looked over the people Sara had gathered so easily, and he felt a warmth for them. They were rallying around her, to inspect this stranger who had moved in on her. That was a part of his maneuver. Her friends had to know him and inspect him, as they accepted that he was there in her house. It had to be clear that he'd moved in.

And he looked at Sara. She was a jewel. Her cheeks were flushed and she was handling it all very well. For a woman like her to suddenly be confronted with such an intrusive man, she was doing brilliantly.

The conversations were light and there was laughter. It pleased Mike that the men eyed him and weighed him and questioned him. The women listened and added questions of their own.

He replied in all honesty, but he didn't really give all the information he could have given. He'd been army for a long, long time. He told stories about other people. He gave names and places and he was never the center of any story. And he encouraged stories in return.

The men helped clear away the meal. The stew was gone. They all complimented him on his cooking.

Mike shrugged. "I learned early to peel potatoes."

And the smokers put on their coats and drifted out onto the porch for an after-dinner cigarette. Dan chided Mike for smoking. Mike said, "One more and I'll quit."

It was an early night for them, being a weeknight. Their guests left with called goodbyes, and it had been a fine evening. Mike was mellow.

When the two were alone, Sara sympathized: "You must be very tired. All the work you've done today! My car—" she didn't actually shudder "—the food. I hope you haven't exhausted yourself." She watched him anxiously.

And Mike realized he'd "recovered" a little fast.

With a mental apology to all mechanics, he assured her, "Taking a car apart is passive work. You just have to know what you're doing. And with the stew, I just dumped it into the pot. That's a fine pot. Salty would love it."

"Who is Salty?"

Mike turned blank eyes to Sara. He'd said Salty's name! He'd avoided mentioning any family names. His glib reply was almost instant. "He does most of the cooking."

"Army? Or at the home?"

"The home." To distract her, he lifted his hands and leaned his face into them to rub it very carefully, avoiding irritating the almost healed scratches.

She said, "You need to get to bed."

He looked at her and saw her concern. It hadn't been an invitation. She was anxious for his health, not his well-being. He couldn't protest. Not yet. For a while longer, he needed her to think he was still a convalescent, still needing care.

He said, "You'll need to drive my car tomorrow."

"It's a good car."

He assured her, "Yours will be almost that good when I get it back together."

She asked cautiously, "Do you know much about cars?"

"Enough." He smiled some more. He was amused by her. What a kind woman. Any other woman would have hit the ceiling when she came home and found her car all over the garage that way.

She mentioned, "You told me you were having a 'last' cigarette when I came home, and you were smoking this evening."

"I forgot."

She amended that. "You can't quit."

"Oh, yes. I can do anything. I'll quit."

"You smell of tobacco."

"I'll shower."

"Your breath—"

"I'll gargle." He headed for the bathroom.

"You don't have to do that."

"I'm going to kiss you good-night."

She lifted her eyebrows in a snooty way. "Oh?"

He stopped and looked back at her. He looked like a dangerous beast that was trying to appear to be a tamed one. He said, "I'll let you sniff me, to be sure I'm pure."

Little licking tremors slithered around inside her. She became owl-eyed and stared at him.

He smiled the faintest bit and went on into the bathroom, as if he were a permanent fixture in that house and it was an ordinary thing that he was there.

She *could* have gone into her room and closed the door. She did not. She moved about, straightening tidy things and listening. The shower ran, then was turned off, and she could hear him gargling. Delicious sneaky flickers stimulated intimate parts of her in anticipation. She would be forced to sniff around him—and to kiss him—in order to test whether he was "pure." Mike? Pure? She seriously doubted it.

When the bath door opened, she stood bravely, her head up, her back straight, braced to endure the testing.

He was wearing Tim's robe and the bottom of his legs and feet were bare. Was he naked under that robe? People were generally naked under their clothing. But a robe could be discarded very easily. She watched him soberly as he approached.

It pleased him to be wearing Tim's robe, because Tim had never been in it with Sara watching. Or had he?

She observed the way he licked his lips and marked that his ears were pricked forward just like a lion anticipating a wildebeest. She saw that happen. He was going to consume her.

He asked, "Ready?"

It would be now. She couldn't breathe, her lips parted and her head wasn't steady, but she didn't retreat. Why not? Well. This wasn't a time for a philosophical self-debate, she'd figure it out later. She waited.

He came right to her and stood before her. He was watching her intently. What did he see?

He saw a rabbit.

She was shivering in little tremors. Was she afraid of him? His face changed. He said in a low voice, "Don't be afraid of me."

That boggled her. Who was afraid? She was excited. She frowned a little.

He reminded her, "You promised to see if I'm pure. Don't you want to test me?" His voice was very low and careful. It was the way a man talked to a chancy beast.

He thought she was dangerous for him? Did he think she would molest him? Well, that was possible. How did a woman go about it? Of course, he had given her permission to sniff around him and taste his mouth for tobacco.

She moved closer, mesmerized by the intentness of his blue eyes, his lash tips that were bleached by the sun, and his sun-streaked hair and brows. He looked like he'd been in faraway places and while he had seen too much, he had survived.

Did she really see that or did she know it from watching CNN?

But he *had* survived.

She went closer and saw that his breathing was unsteady. He had his hands in the pockets of the robe and he stood flat-footed and braced.

Did he think she would fling herself on him?

He watched her shyness. But she *was* closer. She moved so slowly, so timidly, that he was careful of her. She could be spooked.

Again, he didn't lean over so that she could reach him easily; he made her stretch up along his body. She carefully held the lower part of her away from him, but his chest loved the sliding feel of hers. And she sniffed along his chin and around his mouth.

Shivers went up him, lifting his hair, and he tingled down his length. His breathing had become erratic and he trembled, but he held firm.

She was a little faint.

His hands went to her sides—to steady her, of course—and his brushing palms almost cupped the sides of her breasts, he was so sneaky.

Then his mouth rooted around, hunting hers, and he kissed her with unbelievable skill and knowledge. Where had he learned that? He moved his mouth a little, and he shifted his body a little, and he gently pulled her waist closer to him.

Her back was still rigidly arched so that her hips tilted away from his, so he had to run one hand down a little from her waist to pull her closer yet.

Although her grip on his shoulders didn't lessen, her startled eyes popped open and she gasped into his mouth, triggering his male throat into automatically making soothing sounds. Although his hands on her waist moved up and down gently, his lower hand pulled her tighter to him so that she wouldn't get away.

With her lower body's intense awareness of him being male, his mouth was coaxing, to placate her and distract her attention. His kisses were sweet sips, but his breaths were scalding steam and he shivered, as if he were freezing. How could that be, with his breaths so hot?

Sara was far out of her depth and floundering. She began to make little squeaks and gasps. She was distressed.

Mike recognized all that. He lifted his mouth and croaked, "Am I pure?"

She didn't know how to reply.

Since she obviously hadn't made up her mind, he kissed her as he wanted. It was torrid, tempting and terrific! He spun her eyeballs and his, too.

Then he released her. There were just things a man had to do. Releasing Sara at that time was one of those horrific responsibilities.

His hands shook and he shoved them into the pockets on the robe and stood solidly, recovering as much as he could under those circumstances.

Sara stumbled over and plopped down on the little sofa. She put her head in her hands and just sat there.

Until she did that, Mike had been concentrating on just standing. Now a really wicked smile began on his mouth and his feverish eyes loved the sight of Sara struggling with her own libido.

She would be his.

He went over and sat beside her. Very gently he lifted her face from her hands and looked into her unfocused eyes. He said gently, "I need a good-night kiss."

He pulled out all the stops and he gave her a killer kiss that was illegal in all the states and in most foreign countries. He just went ahead and did that. He kissed her twice. He stopped only because he couldn't handle another.

It was with great nobility, and an even greater craftiness, that he then released her and went stiffly to his room. He removed the robe and got into that pristine bed naked. And he lay there. His second hunger was for a cigarette. He could satisfy that one. He got up and went to the window and sat there smoking about ten "last" cigarettes.

It was obvious he'd have to buy another carton.

He heard her alarm the next morning. He got up and pulled on trousers and shirt and went out to fix the coffee and start her breakfast. What did she eat?

It wouldn't matter. He'd kiss her and she wouldn't realize what she was eating.

His stroll to the bathroom door was a little cocky. He tapped and slightly opened the door to her gasp. He didn't poke his head inside, but just asked, "Eggs and bacon?"

"What?"

She wasn't a morning person. "Eggs and bacon for breakfast?"

"Okay."

He nobly closed the bathroom door and went back to the kitchen. He got everything ready and went to see if she was. Ready for him? Yeah. He took a steadying breath. The bath door was open and the steamy air was wafting around the short hall. He tapped on her door.

"Yes?"

"How ready are you?" His eyes tilted and he smiled to himself.

"Just a minute."

He went back to the kitchen. Her days were numbered. He poured her coffee and began the bacon.

"This is very nice of you," she said, as she came into the kitchen putting on an earring.

She looked so fresh and rested that he frowned at her. He felt as if he'd been pulled too quickly through a board's knothole.

She said, "I don't eat bacon and eggs. I just have cereal."

"Coffee isn't any good for you." He said that. Old Caffeine Brown said that. Caffeine Brown, for whom the army had had to ship one whole cargo plane full of coffee to the Gulf, had said coffee wasn't any good for Sara Benton.

"A new study says coffee is probably good for you."

"Who did the study?"

She looked up from her cup. "Coffee brokers?"

"You got it."

"What do you drink?"

He smiled. "Coffee." He monitored her eating the bacon and eggs with honey toast, and he noted she wore no lipstick. "I'm glad you haven't put on lipstick yet."

She glanced up at him again.

"I'd hate to smear it when I kiss you goodbye."

She put down her cup precisely, and mentioned, "I do believe you're getting stronger."

He laughed. He bit his lip and did try not to, but the laughter bubbled out and he looked at her.

Looking everywhere but at him, she said prissily, "I've been keeping track, and you've had more kisses than you're supposed to have had in this time frame."

"How many was I supposed to've had?"

"None. We aren't really acquainted."

That made him laugh again.

"You were up smoking all night long." She threw that in. She'd slept like a log.

With guilty knowledge, he defended: "One last cigarette."

"I heard you."

A little pushy, he asked, "When? What time?"

Evasively, she declared, "And I heard you coughing."

He did hesitate as his computer mind whirled and clicked away and he came up with: "There's a piece of shrapnel that's pressing on my bronchial tube that irritates it."

She narrowed her eyes.

He widened his with such innocence.

It was like observing a pirate who has sworn on his honor.

Seven

———

As Sara stared so soberly at Mike, her expression changed a little and she asked with serious quickness, "Where did you get the money for all that meat yesterday?"

"Hmm?"

"You said your pay hadn't caught up with you and you'd have to sleep in your car. That meat was expensive."

He winged it. How civilian was she? "That was my per diem."

"What is that?"

"Daily food ration."

"Oh." She assimilated his response and said again, "Oh." And she nodded as if his words had explained everything.

She was a civilian.

She glanced at him and her eyes were big. "I'd just wondered—" she gestured as if that explained her words "—how you'd managed," she elaborated needlessly. Then she added honestly, "I didn't understand."

Magnanimously, he said in a kind way, "That's okay."

"I didn't mean to imply that I thought you'd... uh..."

"Lie?"

She shook her head. "You wouldn't."

He didn't deny that he would lie, he just looked gravely innocent.

"I must get to school."

"I'll be close around, in the garage, if you should need me for anything."

"You should probably go back to bed."

He blinked.

"You need the rest."

"I'll do that."

She smiled.

He stood up and held the back of her chair. She did rise. It was automatic. He expected her to stand up, so she did. He didn't move out of her way, and she looked up at him. So, of course, he kissed her. He wrapped his arms around her and he—really—kissed her.

Her hair had to have flown out in all directions and her body must have been buffeted as she fought against the strong wind that tested them. She had to cling and wiggle to fight to stay close to him.

He lifted his mouth and gazed at her lying in his arms, inert, with large stunned eyes looking up at him. Her mouth was red and her cheeks pale.

She slowly stood on her own feet, concentrating on putting them firmly righted, soles down on the floor, and she pulled down her skirt and tidied her blouse and tucked it in more firmly. She moved her skirt so that the zipper seam was back as it was supposed to be, and then she put her hands to her hair. It was a mess. Her hands knew that. Her lips formed the words, "I need my jacket."

"I'll get it."

"It's in my room." She turned and managed to walk back to her room, and she had enough sense to look into the mirror but she only poked at her hair. Blindly, she took a plaid jacket from her closet, and it was just fortunate she was wearing a navy skirt and the two garments didn't clash.

Holding doors for her, Mike walked beside her out to his car and mentioned, "I'm glad you didn't put on lipstick yet."

And darned if he didn't kiss her again! The very same way. He did that and expected her to drive a car? He was a madman.

He put her into the car, apparently considering that she was capable; and since he thought so, she drove and kept on driving until she stopped. She looked around and found herself in the school's parking lot, having arrived safely.

Meanwhile, Mike tidied up the house. Then he went to a bank for change. He found a public phone that was discreet and he called his brother Rod at his place of business over in Fort Wayne.

Rod asked, "Where are you?"

"I'm still in Byford. I've lucked into moving in with the third-grade teacher."

Rod was impressed. "That quick?"

"Naw," Mike was innocent. "She guessed that I'm an orphan and indigent, and I didn't correct her."

Rod laughed.

"—and I was wounded over in the Persian Gulf, on the other side of the world, in the defense of my country which is here on this continent. She swallowed it."

"I can't believe this."

"I can't either. I'm walking on eggshells. Women are nerve-racking."

"How old is the innocent?"

"Now that's a surprise. She's thirty-five."

"She's leading my little brother astray?"

"You won't believe her. I think she's legit. I'm checking her out."

"If she believes you're an orphan and indigent— Now, Mike, who's the fooler here?"

"I am. But I have a toehold. I have to know about this one. She could be real."

"Do some serious checking. Sometimes—"

"Yeah. I know. Cheryl."

"Yeah."

So Mike dangled the bait. "Why don't you come over? You ought to meet her. I've allowed her to believe I lived in an orphanage. She knows Salty was one of the cooks."

Rod laughed, but he took the dangled bait. "Well, actually, saying that isn't too far off. Don't get too tangled up in lies. If this is real, you don't want to disillusion her. You don't want to have to justify too many loose ends."

"Come over for lunch. It would be good to have you help me with her car."

"What's the matter with her car?"

"Nothing, really. I took it apart yesterday. She's driving mine."

Rod's laughter was good in Mike's ear. "I'll be over this noon."

"I'll take you by the school so you can take a look at her." Then he asked Rod to bring along a box of condoms. He explained, "I know that's rude, but everyone in Byford knows I'm staying at her house. I can't buy any here."

"Now, Mike, you be careful."

"I intend doing that. That's why I'm asking this favor of you. If I should be confronted by a miracle opportunity, I want to be prepared. Okay?"

"Done."

And Mike gave Rod directions on how to get to Sara's house.

Then Mike called his commanding officer down in Texas, who came on the phone and asked, "You okay?"

"Pretty good. I just wondered how many calls you've had about me."

"Three, so far."

"Oh, yeah? From who?"

"The principal, Mrs. Atwood, who was cautious, the TV station, and the CHAMPUS doctor, who was nosy."

"What'd you tell him?"

"Nothing voluntarily, I just replied to questions. That you're legit and a good man." He laughed dirty. "If the doc only knew what a hell-raiser you are."

"I?" Felicia's influence was responsible for the single word's perfectly made shocked sound.

"You, you desert rat. You owe me."

"Thanks, Captain."

"Let me know what happens there in Byford. They must have you sitting on a pillow with feather fans."

"Not yet. They're going to have a town meeting this weekend. It's really an outpouring for all the guys that went over to the Gulf. Even you."

"Tough. But a guy has to do his share and accept that others must stay on base and handle the sticky routine."

"You're appreciated in many ways. Don't ask for a list until I'm more agile mentally."

That made the captain laugh again. "Keep your nose clean. I don't want to have to come up there to bail you out of anything."

"I'm pure."

"You are a good man. I didn't lie. Take care of yourself, Mike. Come back well."

"Thanks, Captain."

Mike hung up and smiled at the phone. Then he looked around Byford and smiled at the town. It was a good town. They cared about their people and they'd checked up on the coyote who'd come into town and spotted the rabbit who was Sara Benton.

Mike went back to her house and whistled as he began to reassemble her car... but not too quickly.

An hour later, Rod arrived. He stood and just looked at the gutted car in Sara's garage and he shook his head. "You're underhanded and shrewd. Wouldn't it be interesting to know what kind of genetic parents you actually had? A highwayman and an innocent maiden?"

"She was probably the highwaywoman."

Rod grinned in agreement. He sighed gustily false. "But a guy has to do what he has to do." Then he chuckled. "I am impressed. This car business was really very clever."

"Next time you come over, wear some grease-accepting clothes, and I'll let you help me."

Rod nodded. "A busman's holiday."

"Yep."

Mike called the school and talked to Sara. "One of my brothers from the home has dropped by. How about going with us to lunch?"

"Aw, heck. I only have twenty minutes."

"We'll bring lunch there and meet you in the parking lot. How about that?"

"I'd be delighted."

After Mike hung up, he turned to Rod and smiled big. "She'd 'be delighted.' How about that?"

"She's a lady."

"That's one of the problems."

The brothers went to a fast-food place and collected a variety of foods, then they drove to the school, and Sara joined them in the car.

She was entertained by the two brothers and they made her laugh. They didn't talk about their early boyhoods or where they'd lived.

Sara got back inside the school in the nick of time, and the brothers returned to her house. It was a pleasant enough day, although rather cool. They kept on their jackets and ended up on the porch, so that Mike could smoke. He'd bought the new carton of cigarettes. And the two talked. They spoke of many things, of their upbringing, of the kids who'd been harbored by Salty and his Felicia, about the state of the union, and about Rod's wife.

And Mike asked, "Who takes care of Cheryl?"

"One of the neighbor women who grew up with her."

"I can't tell you how sorry I am for you."

"—and her."

"Yeah."

It had been a long, long time since either had expressed or shared so much, and their lengthened visit was very satisfying for them both. Rod told his brother, "She's something, that Sara. You're a smart man to find out about this."

Mike replied, "I walked into that room and she was there. It spooks me. I kept having to just stop and look at her. I didn't think I was seeing right. You ought to see her with the kids." And he told Rod the story of the mouse, how Sara was revolted by it, but that she couldn't allow him to flush it away.

So Rod was still there when Sara came home. As she exited Mike's car, she did glance at the shambles still in her garage. To her unpracticed eye, it seemed that nothing had been done about her car, but she saw Rod was still there, that he was more relaxed than he'd been at noon, and that Mike's eyes were tired.

She invited Rod to stay to supper and briefly wondered if she would then have two house guests? But he declined supper. He said he had to be getting back to Fort Wayne and, saying his goodbyes, he hugged his brother tenderly.

That touched Sara's heart. Such big rough men, and they hugged each other with such kindness. And she considered that Rod hadn't said he had to get "home," only that he had to return to Fort Wayne.

As Rod drove away, they waved their goodbyes, and Mike felt that being half a couple felt very natural. He watched Rod's car on down the street and then he turned to Sara. "Come inside." He opened the door.

She walked through asking, "*Now* what have you taken apart?"

"I'm working on you. I need to be kissed. I saw you all through the lunch hour and not once did you kiss me."

She pinched her mouth and turned her head busily so that she didn't have to reply, but she did smile.

"You find that funny?"

She tried to stop her smile, but her eyes sparkled.

So he turned her to him, put his arms around her in a very greedy way and he kissed her until she was faint. Then he released her and moved slowly away, his hands seemingly casually stuffed in his trouser pockets.

Sara couldn't breathe at all. She was either susceptible to or allergic to his kisses. Both ways, she was wrecked. She stood where he'd left her.

She couldn't believe any man would kiss a woman that way and then release her and walk away.

She stood, wondering if there was some reason for him not to...for him to...maybe he...couldn't? How could she possibly ask? It would be terrible for a man to say that he could not. But he didn't kiss as if he weren't interested.

He had trembled! It shocked her to remember that.

She'd forgotten he was a convalescent! She wasn't helping him any. He probably was so weakened by his wounds that he didn't dare—uh—expend his energy.

She needed to feed him up and make him strong...enough. She pushed her hair back and straightened her clothing. "I need to go grocery shopping. Is there anything you'd especially like to eat? Anything you craved over in the Gulf?"

He looked at her and thought, A woman.

She smiled. "Another raw steak? I'll get you some beer. Do you like any other liquor?" Candy's dandy but liquor's quicker.

"Beer."

"Why don't you nap while I'm gone? I'll make a pork chop casserole. It won't be long."

"Want me to go along?"

"No. Lie down and rest. I can see you're tired."

Tired! Not *that* tired.

She went into the kitchen and pulled some pork chops from the freezer, and thawed them in the microwave as she gathered the other ingredients. She put the thawed pork chops into the skillet and browned them nicely. Then she lined the casserole dish with them and added potato and apple and onion halves. She heated equal amounts of apricot jam and water in the skillet and poured it over the casserole before she covered it and put it in the oven to bake.

Mike took her advice and went into his room— His...room. It had become his? He licked his lips and took off his shoes and trousers before he lay down and pulled the coverlet over him. He was asleep in seconds.

He awakened as his car was driven back into the drive. He got up immediately and pulled his trousers back on and stuffed his feet into his shoes as he was zipping up. He got almost to the car before she got out of it. And he carried in the groceries and then a *case* of beer!

She expected him to stay long enough to drink a case of beer? His nerves relaxed a little.

Their supper was superb, but the phone calls began again. Herbert's parents had to tell them the mouse had changed their son's life. Teddy was there and was spending the night. The two were building an initial maze for the mouse.

The mayor called to say the town meeting would be that Saturday noon.

And Tim came by....

Sara went to the door, and Mike stayed sitting at the table. He leaned back in his chair and was patient. He said to Sara, "If he's going to visit, you ought to sit down and eat—before your food gets cold."

That tossed the guilt ball into Tim's lap. He was intruding.

Tim observed, "You're still here?"

And Mike replied, "Want a beer? Sara got me a case." He'd gently emphasized the last word. He allowed that stated amount to sink into Tim's awareness.

It did. Tim looked soberly at Sara, who had reseated herself and was obeying Mike's admonition that she should eat her dinner. She didn't offer Tim a place or invite him to join them.

Mike felt sorry for the guy. But not too sorry.

Marilyn dropped by. "Hi, Tim, I saw your car and knew you were here. How's the hero?" She smiled at Mike.

Sara asked, "Would you like a beer? Mike just offered Tim one."

"No, I need some wine for Sally's shower. I just came over because I thought maybe after Tim's through visiting here, he'd help me pick out something nice for that occasion."

Offhandedly Sara said, "Tim knows wines."

Mike smiled in a neutral manner.

Tim said to Marilyn, "Okay."

Marilyn asked, "Now?"

Tim took a last look at Sara, and when she said nothing but continued to eat, Tim said, "Yeah."

Mike told Sara, "Sit still. I'll let them out."

He did that.

When he returned to the table and was again seated, Sara gave him a glance and mentioned, "You hustled them along."

"Yeah." He admitted it. "Tim needs to know you're not available to him. Marilyn will be just right for him."

"Now, how could you know that?"

"I heard Dan Hobart say something along those lines."

That made Sara curious. "When did you talk about Tim to Dan?"

"I don't believe it was said to me," he lied. "As I recall, I just overheard something along these lines last night. Maybe someone said something about their being suited. Maybe that was it?" Adroitly Mike changed the subject. "Where are your people?"

"Gone. Dad left when I was five."

"Where is he?"

"We've never known. He just ... disappeared. We always expected him to come back. But he never did."

"That must have been tough."

"I was too young. But my mom really missed him. She'd come home from work and sit by the window, and she'd look out now and then, as if she might see him coming back."

"And your mom?"

"She died in my last year of high school. She'd really worked hard to keep this house. To make a life for us."

"No other kin?"

"Not that we ever knew."

"So. We're both orphans."

"Did that bother you?" She waited for his reply.

"I don't know. When I understood that people had parents, I tried to get along until mine would come and get me."

"If they had, your life would have been different. Maybe better, maybe worse."

Mike nodded. "Then... after I got to... the home, I gave up on them. I quit waiting."

Sara shrugged in agreement. "You adjust. People do."

"I'm not sure I ever did."

"You've made a good life for yourself. One you can look at with pride."

"I'm not sure I feel as if I've really... lived a life."

"Ahh."

He thought maybe they were getting into something much too serious and deep, so he looked at his watch. "It's been hours since you kissed me. I need a kiss."

She tilted up her nose. "I've already allowed you more than you deserve."

"You're a witch. You've enchanted me to want your kisses, then you deny me. You're a torturer." He shoved his chair back and stood up with his hand out to help her up. "Stand up. You might just as well. I need a kiss."

She picked up the plates and stood up to take them to the kitchen. She gave him a snooty, independent look as she passed him.

So he helped clear the table and straighten the kitchen. He put the soap in the dishwasher and started it. Then he had the gall to sweep the floor.

She started to the other room, and he made short shift of the sweeping and put the broom away quickly in order to follow her. He caught her in the middle of the living room.

And he kissed her. He put his bondage arms around her and took possession of her, kissing her witless. Then he groaned and shuddered and hugged her. He kissed her more seriously, more gently. More hungrily. He lifted his mouth and put his face along her ear and exhaled his steaming hot breath as he growled, "You're driving me crazy."

"You're not helping me a whole lot either."

"Are you complaining?"

"I don't know exactly what you're trying to do to me, but you absolutely wreck me with the kind of kisses you give me."

"I'm not 'giving' them, I'm *taking* them."

She blinked and frowned. "Oh."

He'd forgotten how literal she could be. He lifted his face until he could look at her and he told her silkily, "I'll give them all back."

He kissed her to incoherence.

He guided her stumbling feet into his room and helped her out of her clothing, whatever it was that was covering her body. Somehow he was also out of his own, and they were together on his bed just as he'd longed to be.

She stiffened and gasped and squeaked and wiggled and clutched.

While he pressed and held and shivered and felt, his hands were everywhere on her, smoothing and feeling and rubbing and touching.

And gradually, gradually her body softened and loosened. Her movements became more languid and voluptuously inviting. Her mouth was coaxing and her hands were beginning to explore timidly.

He sweat. He gasped and his breaths became labored. He tensed to iron and his hands became rougher, his mouth moved to her throat and then sought her breasts more earnestly. He squeezed and lifted them to his mouth and he suckled more strongly.

His fingers stroked her heat, encouraging her. He took her hand and put it on him and her hand was startled and didn't know how to act. He showed it. It became intrigued and about set him off.

He got out of bed, and was so thrilled by her quick protest that he leaned back to kiss her before he got his war bag from the closet. He was grateful for Rod's resupply of his scarce hoard.

She braced herself up on her elbows to watch him, and he smiled at her tumbled hair and her alluring, selectively reddened nude body. He took out the condom, released it from the foil and expertly rolled it on his eager shaft.

She was as owl-eyed as she'd ever been, as he came back to her. She had cooled. He noted that and took the precious time to relight her timid fires. He appeared to be in no rush at all. That was brilliant acting on his part, because she had him wild with his own surrender to her lure.

Her rekindling took a while. With his getting the condom, she knew how serious the act had become. He would have her.

He gradually recaught her interest. As her tenseness again loosened and she began the slow movements of enticement that were the automatic indications of need, he deliberately led her further along the sensual paths of rapture, giving her teasing glimpses of the ecstasy to come.

His kisses were no longer greedy, they were soft and sweetly deep as they lured her mouth to clever tender matings. Her own body filmed in the sexual heat, and with its hot sheen their hands slid very easily in appreciative exploration.

He rubbed his afternoon prickly beard along her heated surfaces in slow swirls, then comforted her abraded flesh with his searing mouth. And he relished looking at her writhing below him on his tumbled bed.

She saw that he was thrilled by her move and she noted that his eyes were bloodshot. She was concerned and asked, "Are you all right?"

"I need you." He chuffed and groaned the simple words.

His big, hot hand parted her knees and he loomed over her. She gasped and her scared eyes should have warned him, but he was so triggered that he went ahead. She was so very tight, but so lubricated by desire that he could push into her sheath. Having accomplished his primitive invasion, he held still.

She had tensed so that she was rigid. He realized that if she had ever had a man before then, it had been too long ago, and she was not used to having sex. It was vital that he control himself . . . if he could.

He managed to switch his thinking from his eagerly embedded sex to his concern for Sara. He leaned on his elbows and clasped her head between his hands. "Are you all right?"

"I thought it would hurt."

"Didn't you know?"

She shook her head.

He kissed her gently. Not her mouth, but her eyes, her temples, her cheeks. Soft sipping kissing, controlling himself with stringent discipline that was almost killing him.

He gently brushed his different chest on her breasts and got an answering slithering movement from her.

Her hands had been stiffly on the front of his upper arms, almost as if to brace him away from her. Now they moved to the backs of his arms.

He gave sweet-tasting kisses to her mouth, and moved to her ear to breathe steam there, to touch her ear with his hot tongue, and he got a response of gasping sighs and a slow sinuous flow of movement.

He smiled inside. He lifted his head and smiled into her eyes. "You're really amazing. You're a wonderful woman. You feel so good to me. Are you okay?"

"I believe this is marvelous. I—could you move just a little?"

He levered up. "Am I too heavy?"

"No!" With her word, her hands clutched him back to her so that he couldn't escape. "Not that way. Down . . . there." And she slid timid hands down his slick, hot back to the top of his buttocks . . . pressing!

She almost set him off. He groaned raggedly, "Oh...yeeessss!" Then he moved sneakily. He moved titillatingly. He moved sensually, wickedly. He pleasured her. He fanned her flames and drove her wild.

When he was fast approaching his very top limit, she gasped. She writhed under him, thrilling him almost mindless. She undulated, causing him to gasp, and she pressed him with her fingertips hoping to get closer! She made all sorts of riveting sounds that set him afire. And they rode the glory road to paradise.

When they lay replete, inert, their breaths still laboring, their minds still swooning, she said, "I can't believe it would be this wonderful."

His eyes were closed. "Yes."

There was a long silence.

"We've been in different beds."

He smiled.

"For two whole nights, we were in different beds."

He muttered, "A sex fiend."

She rolled up on her elbow. "I should have known you'd be like this when I saw you come through the door. You scared my stomach even then!"

"Which door?"

"At school."

"You'd have jumped me then?"

"Well . . . I probably would have invited you down to the teachers' lounge."

"That would have been more discreet than the bare floor."

"You'd have gone with me?"

"To the ends of the earth." His eyes were still closed.

"What a pushover!"

He barely nodded. "With you. How'd I do? I can't remember ever making love before. Was I any good? Any complaints?"

"Let's do it again."

"I've been lured into the den of a sex maniac? I'll die happy."

"I'll be careful."

He opened one eye and regarded his love. She had a little smile on her mouth and her hair was dampened by sweat and tousled. Her breasts were still reddened from his attentions. She was enchanting. "You're a witch."

Eight

Mike didn't know anything more until the next morning. Sara's alarm went off in her room, and he turned over to get up—and she was there in bed with him!

The shock jolted through his body and concentrated rigidly. He gasped and put unbelieving hands on her, as if to touch a dream. She opened sleepy eyes and smiled up at him.

She was naked. So was he. How convenient! He left the bed for a condom and almost botched the first one. He was ignited. He got back on the bed and his kiss was enflaming. He was busy with her, far beyond her own arousal. He greedily fed on her and his hands were scandalous.

She laughed in her throat! That sent him over the edge and he didn't wait for her. He took her and rode to glory all by himself.

Expended, he lay on her, gasping, his breathing erratic and his heart running around inside his chest, trying to escape.

She was tolerant. She stretched full-length under his flaccid body and yawned. She said, "There are blankets in the chest. You didn't have to use your battered body to warm me in the night."

"Umm." He was still trying to coordinate his basic life support—like swallowing and pumping blood correctly, just the little things. But he did realize that she was being droll. She was teasing him!

He levered up onto his elbows with great unappreciated effort and he looked at his love. "Sassy." He could only manage that one word. He rolled over sideways, separating from her, and he went back to sleep.

He didn't waken until after ten, when she called to check on him. He stumbled to the kitchen phone on the ninth ring and questioned, "Yeah?"

"I got you up?"

And he laughed.

"Woll, you waken cheerfully. Are you all right?"

"Better." His voice was smoky and wicked.

"I'll be a little late. I have to stop at the boutique and see if I can find a suitable dress for Saturday. And I'm going to call for an appointment with an allergist in Fort Wayne."

"What's the matter?"

"I want to see if I can be desensitized to cigarette smoke."

"Aw... honey..."

"If they can desensitize someone to snake venom, surely they can have a solution to cigarettes."

"Honey—"

"There's some pasta in the freezer. We'll have that. Don't do too much. Get in a nap."

"I can't sleep alone any more."

She laughed.

"You laugh that way and my hair stands on end, too."

Her laughter, then, was different.

After his breakfast, he put on a jacket and went out to survey her car. And he began to work on the parts, cleaning them and oiling things and doing a really masterly job of it.

Dan Hobart stopped off on his way from the hospital to his office. "I had to see how you're doing." He looked around at the still-strewn car pieces. "I can't believe how clever and sly you are. This was brilliant. She can't possibly throw you out."

"She could have called the police and sued."

"Sue a war hero? Don't be stupid. But don't be evasive and clever with me, how are you getting along with her?"

"She's going to get an appointment over in Fort Wayne to see an allergist to desensitize her to cigarette smoke."

"My God. You've hooked her!"

Mike was gloomy. "I'll probably have to quit smoking."

Dan added, "Because they can't desensitize her." It wasn't even a question. Dan already knew that it was impossible.

"Yeah. But look at the burden to my soul. She intended to go through all that for me. Now I'll have to quit." He sighed in great melancholy.

"Is this one of the times that try a man's soul?"

Mike nodded and lit another cigarette.

Dan was helpful. "You could ease off slowly."

Mike slid a disbelieving glance over at the doctor. "Let me guess, you've tried quitting."

"I'm living proof it can be done. Like Mark Twain, I've done it a thousand times. It's easy."

"I've some nicotine pills that will help. It really is an addiction. Nicotine withdrawal isn't quite as bad as a heroin addict's."

"Tell me about it." He was being a little snide.

"Let me help you. We can. It still isn't easy, but there is help for you."

"Okay. I'll come over tomorrow."

"One last day?" Dan shook his head, but his tone held sympathy.

Gloomily, Mike explained, "I have to take another look at Sara."

Dan made a chiding sound, but he patted Mike's shoulder. "I hope you stick around Byford."

"I'm army for a while longer."

"I still hope you'll be around."

"I probably have no choice." His voice wasn't at all cheerful.

"You're a good man."

"My captain told you that."

"Yeah, but I've had it proven to my own satisfaction."

Dan left, reminding Mike to come to the office and get a patch to help him quit smoking.

Mike waved him off...and lit another cigarette. He leaned a hip on the car's fender and contemplated the still bare tree limbs on that chilly March day, and he considered just how addicted he was to cigarettes.

But the thing was, he could become addicted to Sara, at least for a time.

Just because she was a bed-willing female? And he remembered how he'd been whammied the first time he'd laid eyes on her. Then he thought of her concern over a repulsively stupid mouse and her endurance at seeing her car gutted.

He took a long drag on the cigarette as his glance was drawn from the bare branches to the striding figure who approached. It was Tim.

Uh-oh. Mike wondered how much of a threat such a confrontation could be. Tim was a little bigger and a little heavier than he, and Tim wasn't rattling around with shrapnel. Watching the big man approach, Mike speculated as to whether Tim knew judo.

Then, as he waited, Mike shifted his feet as he moved away from the littered ground in case they should fight.

Tim noted that. He came within about six feet of Mike and stopped. They stood and observed one another. Tim asked, "Are you serious about Sara?"

"Why do you ask?"

"You have to know I had her pegged for myself. I need to know that you aren't just fooling around."

Since he couldn't agree to step aside, he offered, "I'm going to quit smoking."

Tim looked at the cigarette still in Mike's hand.

"I know. It isn't easy. I have to gear up for quitting."

"You'll quit until you have her nailed, and then you'll start again. She can't take cigarette smoke."

"I know."

"You risk her health when you smoke."

"That's why you quit?"

And Tim was grim. "Yes."

"I can understand it. I may not be the man you are, but you have to understand that you aren't for Sara. If you were, it would have been apparent between you before I ever showed up. You're a good man. You're such a good man that you scare the hell out of me, that Sara will compare us and find me lacking."

Tim stared.

Mike stared right back.

"You admit I'd be better for her!"

"I admit it—to you." Mike clarified it.

"I could tell her you said so."

"It wouldn't do you any good."

The shadow of pain that went over Tim's face was echoed inside Mike's compassion. "I know that you've loved her for some time."

Tim warned, "Don't you ever harm her."

"I wouldn't."

Tim looked at Mike for a telling minute of dire threat, then he turned and stalked away.

Mike watched after the man and felt his turmoil. Pity lurked in Mike and he slowly shook his head with sympathy. There was no way that he'd give up Sara yet. He took a last drag on that cigarette and tossed it away. Then he had to go over and step on it because the leaves were brittle.

At lunch, Mike listened to the radio and learned that the weather would change. A spring storm was due and there could be a light snow. He went through the coat closet and took a coat over to Sara at the school.

Having gotten permission, he walked down the hall. Mike returned the greetings of one kid and then a teacher. Watching the pair out of sight in opposite directions, Mike knocked on Sara's door and waved a big hand over the glass panel, but he waited in the hall.

She came out of her room to him and smiled. He checked the halls. They were empty. So he kissed her.

With heavy eyelids, she mentioned, "You may not kiss me in the morning before I leave for school—I wore the wrong jacket today."

He looked at the green jacket, and it looked okay to him. "What's wrong with that jacket?"

"It goes with another skirt."

"Well, you've just discovered that it goes with that one too." He looked up and down the empty hall, reached for her and he kissed her as he wanted.

She was lax in his arms and formed the words slowly, "You must not kiss me that way, here. I take too long to recover."

"Good."

"Why didn't you notice my garter belt last night?" She really hadn't intended to ask that.

He tried to remember. "What garter belt?"

"My red one."

"Do you have it on now?"

"Yes."

"I'll check it out when you come home."

"Mike!" she chided.

"What're'ya upset over?"

"You're scandalous."

"Because I'm going to check out your garter belt? What's salacious about that? I'll just...lift your skirt...and—"

"Hush!"

He whispered the rest. "—and look."

She laughed silently, but she blushed scarlet.

He released her and patted her bottom. His eyes glinted, as he told her, "I'll look forward to seeing you at home." And he left her standing there.

He walked away, thinking, "I called her house 'home.'" At the corner of the hall, he looked back and again she was watching after him. He stood and looked back at her and he smiled. He threw her a kiss. She reached up and caught it. She had to jump in order to do that. He laughed.

She might be literal, but she had humor.

With the threat of worse weather, it could get too cold to work on her car, so he had to reassemble it. He did that with dispatch, and then drove the car to a do-it-yourself car wash and cleaned it thoroughly inside and out.

He returned it to her garage and went inside to see about the pasta. He checked the fruit and made a salad. And he organized their supper. He blessed Salty for giving all the kids training in basic cooking.

He was finished by the time the storm blew Sara into the house. She slammed the door and looked at him. "My car's back together!"

"Yeah." He grinned.

"Or did you just throw away all the parts that were scattered around?"

"You can try it."

She shivered. "It's freezing out there!"

"It's March."

"But spring break is next week!"

"We'll go to San Antonio."

"What a good idea!"

"I'd take you down to Padre Island, but the vultures from colleges will be there, and they'd—let's see that garter belt." He took her coat from her shoulders.

"What an odd sentence!"

"I'm an odd man. I like asking to see garter belts."

"You're a lecher?"

"I never was, before this. It has to be Byford's drinking water...or something." He licked his lips. "Okay. I'm braced. Let's see that red garter belt."

"Here in the kitchen?"

"You've never made love on a kitchen table?"

"Have you?" She was shocked.

"No, but we could try it. Let me see that red garter belt."

"Not now."

"We need to talk." He took her arm and hurried her along, hovering over her, making her walk too fast and looking down at her chest as she jiggled with her quick steps. He smiled like a wolf and patted her bottom. Then he left his hand on her bottom because it was jiggling too.

She said, "You're very forward, Sergeant."

"Yeah."

They had reached his room.

"What are we doing here?"

"We're going to see the red garter belt."

"Oh, that." She twitched and considered and looked around, unseeing as she pretended to consider his request.

He went over to the bed and lounged on it. "First the jacket."

"Take it off?"

"One thing at a time."

"Why, Mike, I can't do that."

"I just want to watch you. I'm depleted and no threat."

She eyed him, unbelieving. But maybe he was telling the truth. He was on convalescent leave. She studied him a minute, then she slowly took off her jacket.

Mike controlled his urgent need to help her.

She slid her skirt off.

He shifted restlessly.

She carefully unbuttoned her blouse, watching her fingers seriously, not knowing to look up at him and flirt or tease.

He coughed.

She discarded the blouse and slowly stood there in her plain white cotton slip.

He could almost see a part of the red shadow of the garter belt. He smiled, his glances busy.

"Are you ready for this?"

Oh, yes, indeed! "Yeah."

She lifted the slip off over her head, and he had to force himself not to leap off the bed.

She stood there in high heels. The garter belt was under utilitarian white cotton panties and she wore a white cotton bra.

She was precious. He smiled at her. "Uh... Let's see if we can get those panties off and leave the belt on."

She looked down. "Really?" She looked up. "It isn't—"

"I'll watch."

She slid the panties down off her hips and paused. She did do that. Her face was the same color as the garter belt and her hands shook a little. She was very earnest. She peeked at him.

He smiled and held still.

She removed the panties, but she took off the high-heeled shoes.

He suggested, as if having just thought of it, "Put your shoes back on."

"Why?"

"—and take off your bra."

She looked up, startled, and her hands covered her white cotton bra. "I can't do *that!* It would be immodest."

"Please. It's a lifetime dream of mine."

And she did consider that. She'd had that red garter belt for three years. She had never discarded it. She'd only had the courage to wear it for Mike, and he'd never even really seen it. She'd worn it for her own courage. Her own feeling of recklessness. Ahh, that was the word.

She looked at him. "Is it for recklessness?"

"No." He was serious. "It's for the aesthetic appreciation of an art treasure."

She stared.

He held very still.

She could understand that. Men did look at pictures of naked women for the pleasure of seeing their forms. Art was often concerned with naked women. Statues. Paintings. "Are you serious?"

He nodded. "I'm a lover of beautiful things, and you are beautiful."

She reached back and undid her bra. And she put her toes into her high-heeled slippers. She leaned over to wiggle out of her bra and about shot his brain right out of his skull. She worked earnestly, not flirting or posing. She was unaware of her effect on him.

He held his breath the entire time. Then he watched, as she straightened up and looked at him. She was uncertain. He was almost overwhelmed. He told her in a husky voice, "You're a man's dream."

"Really?" She looked down at herself and put out her hands with the palms up. "This?"

"Yeah. They have to make do with other women, but men all dream of you."

She laughed and shook her head in disbelief, sure that he was teasing. His face stayed serious. She watched him a minute, then asked, "Okay?"

"Yes."

So she busily picked up her discarded clothing *and turned to leave the room!*

He rolled up onto his hands and knees to exclaim, "Where're you going?"

"To get dressed." She glanced back at him.

"Come here."

She stopped and just looked at him.

"Don't you realize what comes next?"

"What?"

"We do." He got off the bed and went to her. He took the clothes from her hand and tossed them aside. He looked down her body. He said, "Wow" very softly. He smiled and hugged her to him, without any thought of the metal that was embedded in his body. He thought of nothing but Sara.

He led her to the bed and laid her down—

"My shoes."

"Leave them on."

"On the *bed?*"

That had obviously been drilled into her head from birth. "Why not?"

"I could hurt you."

He paused, then he straightened up so that he could look down at her. She was serious. He was so charmed by her. He very carefully leaned down and removed her shoes and put them on the bedside table next to his cigarettes. Then he looked at her.

Other than blushing rather painfully, she allowed that. Her face was serious. Her passion sleeping. She was holding still for his pleasure.

He closed his eyes and tilted his head back, seeking control and he breathed her name.

His lovemaking then wasn't the rowdy session her garter belt had triggered. It was tender, gentle love. It was so filled with worship that the garter belt was incongruous.

He very slowly caught her sensual attention and led her past her shyness as he built her interest to passion. Then he made love to her. He was not a man who simply used women.

If Sara had had no other yardstick to judge him, his conduct then would have given her his measure. He was a man in the true sense of that meaning.

Her first indication of that had been his replies to the class's letters, the second was his visit to them and the third stunning, heart-touching one was that he'd memorized all their names.

Her regard was such tender response. She touched him with such gentle hands that she lifted his hair right off his head. And her lips were soft and welcoming. Her body was responsive to his advances, and his hands relished her.

The texture of his body was so different that to have his hairy chest against her sensitive nipples was thrilling to her, and she blushed with her pleasure. And he deliberately rubbed himself against her so she would feel the difference.

His mouth was bold and she was somewhat startled, but the sensations were phenomenal. She gasped, and her movements became sinuous. She squeaked, and he had to catch those sounds in kisses that were deep and earnest.

He led her down the enticing primrose path to lurid pleasure, and she danced along with him in rapture.

As they lay replete and contented, she asked, "Have you any faults?"

"Other than smoking?"

"Yes."

"I'll hide them carefully and only practice them when you won't know. I want you to believe that I'm perfect."

"If you were perfect, I'd be uncomfortable with you. I am not."

He grinned, bit his lip to stop it, but he laughed in disbelief. Then, to tease, he inquired, "Outside of being remarkably literal, what are your faults?"

"I am, on occasion, very impatient."

"No. You're the most patient woman I've ever known."

"How many have you known?"

"Only you, just lately."

"Have . . . you had a . . . great many women?"

"No."

"Why aren't you married?"

He thought, frowning a little, and then he said the obvious, "I don't live the kind of life a woman would want to share." He was completely serious. It was what he believed.

"Miiikkke," she pinched her mouth, to hide her disbelieving smile.

"Now why do you say my name that disbelieving way?"

"You are a marvelous man. Women would notice. They would have clamored for your attention."

"I'm a noncommissioned officer and I've never wanted to be anything else. We don't make a whole lot of money. We move around. Army life can be a hardship for a woman. It was a life I wanted."

He didn't want a woman permanently? She drew back just a little. "I see."

Not aware of her withdrawal, Mike explained further, "I'm good with motors. Salty taught us to know machinery. The army uses all kinds of things that need fixing, and I can fix just about anything."

She smiled a little. "So my car was never in any real danger?"

He grinned. "When I let you out of my bed, you can go out and start it and see how it runs."

"If the last less-than-twenty-four hours are any indication of your activity, you are also skilled beyond motors."

He leaned over her and gently ran a big rough-skinned hand up her bare body. "You got something that needs fixing?" His voice was heavy with innuendo.

Literal, she replied, "My iron."

"Irons don't have motors."

"The vacuum cleaner."

"I can tackle that."

"How about a computer?"

"No motor."

"Well, at least you're good for something."

He gasped. "You don't think I'm a good lover?"

"I haven't had any other experience. For all I know, all men are that good."

"So you think I'm good?"

"It's just amazing!" Then she had to ask, "How do I compare with your...other lovers?"

"What other lovers?" He was all innocence.

She chided, "You knew what to do."

"I read a lot."

"My goodness, what sort of books tell you about—the things you did to me?"

"Veerrrryyy interesting ones." He automatically reached over for his pack of cigarettes, then hesitated.

She saw the hesitation.

He pulled his hand back and looked at her.

She regarded him with serious eyes.

He put a tender hand to her face. "What's the matter?"

"I called the allergist over in Fort Wayne and asked about being desensitized . . . for tobacco." She looked down, her face sad. Then she looked up at him with her blue, blue eyes and she went on: "They said they couldn't do it. When they used to try, the people got cancers where the shots were given."

He said, "Humph." And he said, "That's sobering."

"Is there any way you could quit? You're risking yourself."

"I'll quit. Dan was here for a couple of minutes this morning. He said he can help me get over the hump."

"For your own sake."

He corrected that. "So I can be around you."

"Oh, Mike." And she hugged him to her soft body.

They left their bed of passion, and she wore the pink lace wrap that she'd once offered to let him wear. In Tim's robe, Mike appreciated seeing her in the pink lace and watched her with a pleased smile lingering on his lips.

They fixed their dinner and she told him what the kids had said and done, and she commented on the slowly developing metamorphosis of Herbert into a real human being. The mouse had begun that, but it was really Teddy who was the normalizing influence. He didn't realize how intelligent Herbert was and therefore Teddy treated that brain as if he were average.

Sara told Mike about the teachers and what they'd said.

He smiled at her and listened and commented, but he didn't share his morning's confrontation with Tim.

He noticed that her tales were always of someone else. She wasn't critical or snide. She was an observer and a relater. She didn't always see subtle humor, but she had humor and told of it. She was a cheerful woman. She cared about the kids and her friends. He found that he wanted her to care about him.

After they'd finished eating, he was restless and moved jerkily and got up for no reason and settled down, to get up again. Restless.

She guessed, "You need a cigarette."

"Yeah." He sighed and twitched.

"Go outside and smoke one. Don't quit until Dan can give you some help."

"I ought to be able to do this by myself."

"It will be better with help."

"I'll go out and jog around the block."

"Are you supposed to?"

"I can go at my own pace."

"From what I've witnessed, you're very fast."

That was so unexpected that Mike put his head back and laughed beyond the humor of it.

She didn't see what was funny, and explained, "You fixed the car today. You put all that back together." It had been an impressive accomplishment, quickly done.

With her word "fast," she hadn't been referring to his seduction of her.

Nine

The next morning, Mike did go over to Dan's office and get the patch to help him quit smoking.

Dan assured him, "Quitting will be one of the most important things you can do for yourself. It takes willpower, but you're a strong man and you can do this. It's something you need to do for your own self."

Mike was dubious and not sure that he really wanted to do something that committed, but he felt he should quit at least for the time he was around Sara.

Dan was solemn, as he said, "Good luck."

That had been the same serious way his commander had said those same words when their jigsaw-puzzle part in the Desert Storm war had begun. They'd gone forward in a convoy, with gasoline and spare parts to keep everything moving. With all those oil wells aflame, trucking oil into the country was the irony.

In Byford, Indiana, Friday came, and the people who had inquired into Mike's plans and felt so familiar as to ask them, began to give Mike some pause in his thinking. And again people came to Sara's house to see them. They felt welcomed to be interested, to question and to judge.

Hadn't he been charmed by their interest just a couple of days ago?

Mike finally faced the fact that everyone was crowding in on him. While he wanted to be with Sara, he wasn't sure he wanted to live with the complication of a woman tagging along after him.

With the loose ties of Salty and the army, he'd been a free, unfettered man all his life long. It had been deliberate. Even at the Browns' home, he had been free. He had simply adjusted to their rules, but his life had been his own. His thoughts had been his own. The extended Browns had been a needed but expendable anchor to the wind.

Even in the army, Mike had been free. He had made his own judgments. Joining had been his choice. He'd worked within the army rules, just as he had worked within Salty's. Both the navy-trained Salty and the army thought alike. Those rules were ones that Mike could tolerate.

But for him to bend to a woman's rules? They were a different race, and for a man, the woman lure was more confining than chains.

If he adopted some kids, he could hire a sitter who would go home when he was there. He wanted no other commitment. All he really wanted was a willing woman, on the side, whom he could visit.

He looked at Sara and thought that might not be a nice thing to do to her.

He cautioned her, "Don't get serious about me. You know that I still have time to give to the army."

"Yes."

"I can't make any commitment."

"I understand."

"What if I left and didn't . . . make it? That could happen, you know."

Her eyes were serious. She replied slowly, but she was honest. "I would grieve for you."

"What if I just . . . didn't come back for you."

"Being with you has been—so different. I'm glad you came here and stayed with me."

"And you wouldn't regret lying with me, making love with me?"

She considered her words very carefully. "I . . . would . . . treasure the memory."

"Would you marry someone else?"

"It would depend on the man." She looked at him with understanding. "You're getting conscience twinges. And you believe I will try to trap you. I wouldn't. You are free." She opened one hand out, palm up, to indicate she was not holding him.

That gave him pause. If she said he was free, under these conditions...then...so was she! She didn't feel committed to him? He frowned at her. Was she just toying with him and experimenting with a man who wasn't local and who would have to leave? Or was it a ploy to make him pay attention and get territorial?

What had he gotten himself into?

She said, "It's probably just as well. We'll enjoy each other until after this weekend, then you can be free to leave."

He stared at her.

She said in a relinquishing way, "You are a wonderful man. Byford will remember you forever. Just that you wrote back to the kids was enough to engrave your name into this town's memory. But to come here and to call the kids all by name was stupendous. You've touched our lives for the good."

"—and your life?"

She smiled and rolled over on his bed. "You're remarkable. I'm glad you came to my house."

"No regrets?"

"Not after a while. I will miss you badly at first. But my memories of you will be so sweet that there won't be any bitterness."

Good gravy. He was stunned. No arguments? She could let him go without any fight at all? Why should he feel so disgruntled?

Now wait a minute. What did he mean by all that? He wanted her to coax him to stay? To coax him into committing himself to her? He was shocked by the very idea.

Then what was he doing, there in her house, ruining her chances with Tim?

Mike faced that honestly. As fine a man as Tim was, he wasn't for her. He'd had over five months to convince her that he loved her, but in that time she still thought of Tim only as a friend. But there were other men in Byford. She should marry and have children. She was almost past the age for that. He shouldn't be taking up her time.

And the fact that he'd moved in on her, deliberately, did niggle at his conscience. He should get away from her and leave her alone.

She yawned and stretched with luxurious pleasure. "I hadn't known that being with a man was soooo nice."

"You're regretting your carefully lived life?"

She tilted her head back and looked smug. "I think you should have come to Byford long ago. I could then have notched my bedpost."

Other men? He was indignant. With some carefully gathered balance, he questioned, "I've made a sex fiend out of you?"

"Quite...possibly." She smiled a cat's lazy smile.

She offended him. He felt the need to protest on the side of morality. *He* did? He'd consider that debate later. He began awkwardly, "Well, now, Sara, you have—"

"Let's do go down south next week. Would you have the time? I would love traveling with a man. I'll pay my half."

That rattled him even more. With a woman along, he'd always paid the freight. "You'd be my guest."

"Your pay hasn't caught up with you as yet."

He looked at her somewhat disgruntled. "I told you that so you'd be sorry for me and let me stay with you."

She was laughing. She was! He frowned at her. There was nothing more irritating than an unpredictable woman.

Her eyes twinkled, and he watched that, distracted. He'd never seen twinkling eyes. Hers did. She looked— He had to hunt for the word and discarded a good many. She was...charming. She was like a flute with a snake. He was the snake.

On Saturday was the big Byford salute to the troops and to the official end of Desert Storm. Rod came over from Fort Wayne and sat with Sara among those in the audience close to the speakers. Sara wore the perfect blue dress she'd wanted to wear for Mike that first day.

And he wore the camouflage desert uniform, the boots and helmet. In them, he was a different man. Sara looked at him and knew him. But he was so formidable that she was especially aware of the fact that he was a part of a distanced, directed war machine that consisted of humans.

A surprising number gathered at the high-school gymnasium, even some of those who'd opposed the war. They hadn't been opposed to the troops, just the war. And like everyone else, they wanted the troops all home again.

After the first protest yellow ribbons were tied outside, there had come a directive for patriotic Americans to all display yellow ribbons in support of the troops and the war. It was done. Then the war was declared to be finished, and the notification came out that the ribbons should be removed. But some American troops were still over there, still not home, and some ribbons remained in place.

The gym floor had been covered with canvas and chairs set up. When people had walked in, they had been handed a little flag and sheets printed with the words of songs. The bleachers and all the chairs were filled. There were TV camera crews and the representatives of the press. There were people standing around the edges. The noise level was high with enthusiastic chatter and the high-school band played wonderfully. Loud.

It began.

The mayor welcomed everyone, "Fellow citizens of Byford, we are gathered to celebrate the return of our troops from the Persian Gulf. We are honored by the distinguished people who have come to Byford to help us in this ceremony."

He then introduced representatives of Indiana's U.S. senators and congressmen, and the state representatives who were present.

All the guests made speeches, and the band played patriotic songs. Some of the people knew the words, but most had to read from the photocopied pages. They all sang along. It was a gala.

And as a token for all who'd been involved in that faraway encounter, Mike was introduced. The place trembled with the yelling and cheering. He had to stand and wait for them to get it out of their emotional storage of worry and anxiety and the need to communicate it. Mike became the recipient. It took a while.

When the crowd finally settled down, Mike thanked them for inviting him to speak. He told how much the letters from Miss Benton's third-grade class had meant to him. And he said what a good town Byford was. They were all lucky to live in such an American town.

They cheered and waved their little flags and they loved him. It was such an outpouring that Mike could feel it surrounding him, and his eyes became teary because it had taken such tragedy to trigger the intense wave of patriotic sentiment. Then he sat down.

The mayor stood up and said, "I am fortunate, indeed, that Mike Brown isn't going to be a candidate for mayor."

And they all laughed. Then they sang "The Star Spangled Banner," and there weren't very many eyes that didn't tear. It was an emotional time.

It was over.

In the slow exodus, people visited and appeared reluctant to let go of the celebration. It seemed they all had to talk to Mike, to touch him or shake his hand.

Mike understood that he was important to them as a symbol of all the others. And he saw Herbert's exuberant parents. Herbert was with them and he *winked* at Mike. Mike laughed in understanding, and then Herbert laughed too.

Rod carefully hugged his brother with some emotion, but he declined the invitation to go back to Sara's house and he left them to return to Fort Wayne.

The lovers finally went back to Sara's and a good many of her friends came by, unable to relinquish the feelings of unity.

Mike was quiet. He sat and watched Sara as she hostessed her friends, and he thought what a unique woman she was.

Along with knowing men, Mike had known women. All sorts. "Good, bad and indifferent." All the contrasts were represented in both genders. The women were of the same variety of characters that covered men, only the women had the feminine version.

And he knew that Sara was special. That depressed him.

That night, in his bed, he said to her, "That blue dress is really something . . . on you."

"I've had it in the back of my closet for months and I wanted to wear it that first day, when we knew you would come to see us."

"Why didn't you wear it?"

"I was afraid everyone would think that I was trying to lure you."

"You weren't?"

"Yes. I wore the red garter belt."

"Now, how was I supposed to know that? How did you intend for me to know?"

"I wore it for recklessness."

That stumped him. "How were you reckless?"

"I brought you home with me."

"I'm glad you did."

"Me, too."

He was in such a strange withdrawn mood. It was she who had seduced him. It was she who teased him to passion. He allowed that. He was so touched by her hesitant explorations, by her blushes and shyness that he was aroused to a need that was different from any he'd ever experienced.

He gave her the freedom of his body and she was curious. He submitted to her pace and didn't hurry her along. He was captured by her gentleness and her humor. She amused him, while his compassion was touched. She was a whole woman.

Their coupling was exquisite. That was an unusual word for Mike. Felicia used it for something that was almost beyond explaining. Sara deserved that word. She was exquisite.

The feel of her body against him was precious. His body reacted with such tenderness. And when they joined their love, he was mesmerized by her, his attention was so concentrated that he wasn't conscious of anything beyond their bed of love.

His hands moved on her with a wonder that he couldn't recall ever feeling before then. Against him was Sara, it was she who sheathed his ardent sex, it was her hands in his hair. He had never been conscious of such an intensity of feeling . . . for his partner in sex—in making love. His concentration had always been on his own desire and its culmination.

Her mouth on his was life-giving, and to be denied her mouth made him restless. Lacking. So his movements, his hands, his mouth were becoming enticing to *her* satisfaction, her pleasure.

He realized something was happening to him. His awareness of her was so unusual. His instinctive self-preservation began to kick in, making the opening up of his emotions retreat.

He was afraid. What was happening to him? He controlled himself, and he made love with great appreciation and skill. The climax was spectacular. But all the while, his emotions were coming back under his control.

He did not recognize it was love. Or perhaps he resisted knowing.

She slept that night in his arms. Their nude bodies sharing his heat. She coughed a couple of times and had to get up and get water. Then she finally had to say in apology, "I need to go back to my own bed."

"Why?"

She gestured helplessly, not knowing how to say it.

"Have I offended you?"

"Oh, Mike. Of course you haven't. But I'm having trouble... the bed smells of smoke."

"My God. I'm sorry, Sara."

She suggested, with a deliberately sly smile and a slight twitch of her body that was scandalous, "Shower and sleep in my bed."

"You scarlet woman!"

"Yes." And she'd laughed in her throat, but she coughed again.

She turned her naked back to him and said, "See you later." She was sassy. Sara? She was turning into a temptress? If he left, whom would she tempt next?

He soaped down and rinsed off like a surgeon before an operation. He also gargled. Then he went into her room, and for the first time he got into her bed. It smelled of her, of her unique fragrance.

She didn't just move over. She curled next to him and she purred. She did. She chuckled in her throat and made "M" sounds and she purred again as her hands and one foot slid on his body and petted him.

He warned her, "Careful. You're making me think you want me."

She laughed that way again.

And he was triggered. Around her, he'd always been halfway there. She stirred his passion like no other woman he remembered.

Before Sara, sex had been a great act. Satisfying. Nice. Relaxing. Needed.

To have her react that way to him was a special welcoming to her bed. She knew that. He did, too. This was her admission that she loved him.

While they'd been in his bed, their couplings had been a surprise, a happenstance, a fluke. But it was different since their lovemaking was in her bed. They lay there in each other's arms and both were aware. Neither mentioned it.

He held her and his body loved being there, holding her. His mind resisted.

But having her was different again. Why that was so, he avoided knowing.

He made love to her and he murmured sounds to her and he said her name in many ways, as their passion mounted and flamed.

It was her greediness that sent him over the edge of control. For a woman who was thirty-five years old and who had only indulged in sex for the last several days, she was a firebrand. And he lost control.

In all his days, in the women he'd had, he'd always been in control. He did this and they responded, he did that and they responded, and he rode them hard.

With Sara, he did this and she did that, and he countered and she did something else entirely. It was like point and counterpoint in fencing, only the game was sex.

She shivered his libido and taunted his sex. She touched him and her touches knocked him sideways in a manner no other woman's touches had managed. He felt as if it were he who was new to lovemaking, it was so different with Sara.

And he held her as he climaxed and rode the wild winds held to sanity only by her arms.

He kissed her in tender sips. He patted her with his big awkward hands. And he cherished her.

He, who had always released himself with a pat on the woman's hip before he had lighted a cigarette, had trouble releasing Sara.

Bemused, he drifted into sleep. That was like lying with her on the lap of Morpheus, secure, protected, sated.

On Sunday morning, they packed up Mike's car and drove south. They had no destination. He gave her an extra set of keys for her purse, "In case—" They drove from a bare-branched, brown grass, cautious promise of spring, into the reality of its fragile beginning and on down into the full bloom of it.

They were companionable. She wasn't too chatty. She watched and enjoyed and shared. She was cheerful and ready to exchange opinions. She was knowledgeable, but not prissy about that. She didn't contradict him or show off. She was simply good company. She was easy to be around. That depressed him a little more.

He told her Desert Shield had been six months of boredom and sand, and the actual war had been a hundred hours of intense pressure. Those left over there had reverted to the boredom part. For him that was explanation enough. They'd been in the known army cliché of "Hurry up and wait."

And it was during their Idyll Trip that he locked his keys inside the car. She was in the bathroom at the motel and he automatically opened her purse to find the spare set. It was then he saw that she carried his picture... laminated. He was stunned. He put it back and returned her purse to its place on the bureau. And he rummaged in his war bag for a pack and went outside to smoke a very serious cigarette.

After the first lungful, he threw it away, put his hands into his pockets and walked slowly up and down the motel sidewalk, deep in blankness.

She had fallen in love with a picture. She was in love with her dream. She didn't know the real Mike Brown—or whatever his name should have been. He was a throwaway child. He thought bitterly: Think of the genes included in that.

He went back into the room and she sniffed him. Then she smiled. "Another try?"

He had to smile back. "Yeah."

"It was a spectacular effort. I was impressed."

See? She didn't even get mad at him for slipping. Her tolerance would be a burden of guilt for all his da—all the rest of the trip.

"I locked the keys in the car. Do you still—"

"In my purse." She gestured. Then she said quickly, "Wait. I'll get them for you." And she hurried to get to her purse first.

She didn't want him to know she carried that laminated picture of him. Now, separately, they both knew that.

They didn't go all the way to the bottom of Texas to the tip of Padre Island. They stopped in some little coastal town that was lazy and very quiet. But the beach was nice.

They lazed in the sun for two days and jumped waves and swam out together in the lush, welcoming Gulf. And Sara picked up shells until her hands were full and she had to add them to his big hands. He was tolerant.

He strung her a necklace of the small fan-shaped shells. They'd been drilled by a greedy sea worm, but inadvertently, the holes were precisely placed to accommodate the thread.

He put it over her head to see how it would hang and added some shells. She had to hunt more, and she was quick and particular to find the perfect ones.

He told her, "No pearls." His tone was solemn.

She lifted the necklace and declared, "These are more beautiful. Look at the colors in this one." She lifted the necklace and displayed the subtle shadings on one of the shells.

"Beautiful," he said, but he was looking at her.

She wore it all the rest of the time, and the sounds as she moved or hurried were the soft clickings of the shells. A different sound.

They went to San Antonio for a day. Sara waited in the car while Mike placed a call from a phone booth. He called Cray, who was an actual child of Felicia and

Salty. He said to Cray, "I'm with a perfect woman, but she is under the impression I'm an orphan and she took me into her house because I had no place to go. Don't louse me up. She thinks you're another from an orphan home where Salty is cook."

Cray said, "Fascinating." And he said, "Do you know about Susanne? We're probably going to get married."

"Is she good enough for you?"

Cray echoed Mike's own words, "She's perfect."

Cray lived in the attic of a small house occupied by six women. Mike and Sara went to see him there. Five of the women ignored Sara and were avidly interested in Mike. Mike didn't notice.

But the sixth woman was Susanne, and Mike noticed her. She loved Cray. That was enough for Mike.

Nothing was mentioned about the Brown family or Salty or Felicia. And Cray was so amused.

Sara thought Cray was a cheerful person. He smiled a good deal and his eyes twinkled. She made that observation to Mike who replied, "Yes."

Then, for some unknown reason, Mike drove over to his army base, there in central Texas, and showed Sara around. It was an A-typical base that followed the pattern. It was well-tended and neat. The trees and lawns were green and pretty. Flower beds thrived. And there were the bluebonnets and other spring flowers, thick and beautiful.

Mike took Sara to meet his captain, Phil Blake, who was not only surprised, the motor-mouth was speechless. He just smiled in an unbelieving manner, but he nodded and was very courteous.

He stared at Sara. She wasn't a sometime woman. She was pink-cheeked with sunburn, her hair was a little windblown and charming, and she wore a string-and-shell necklace with—élan. She was something special. Where had Mike found her? Out of the clear blue, the captain said, "Mike's a good man."

Sara responded with, "Byford was charmed by him. They gave him a salute and most of the town showed up."

"Really?" And he looked to Mike for some explanation as to why a town honored him that way.

Mike's face was stony and uncommunicative.

"It even made the Fort Wayne papers and was on all the surrounding TV stations. He was brilliant."

"We'd like to see the articles," Captain Blake resisted insisting. "What's the paper's name?"

"The *Bugle*."

Phil laughed heartily, more than was necessary, and commented, "Perfect name to report on any army man."

Sara blinked, as she sorted his words.

So the captain expanded his words a little, "You know, an army bugle?"

Although Sara thought that was funny, Mike only endured.

After they left the captain's office, Mike showed Sara the modest wooden duplex where he lived. It was plain and utilitarian. It appeared to her to be a place to sleep, not to live. And she supposed that was really what it was. A harbor, not a home.

He showed her the field where they drilled and he showed her the motor pool.

He introduced her to men and several women who were there working on army vehicles that looked a whole lot similar to what Mike had done to Sara's own car. The people were all startled by Sara being there, and they were careful in their replies. They smiled and their eyes sparkled, but they shot glances at one another as if they could hardly *wait* to discuss the fact that Mike had brought a woman on the base.

With that side trip out of their way, the couple had to drive almost straight back to Byford in order to arrive there on Sunday. Sara had to be back in class on Monday.

The magic week was over. And Mike estimated that in that time he'd chewed over forty-nine thousand sticks of gum.

Sara was so tired that night that Mike didn't ask her to love him. He lay in her bed, holding her quietly, and she slid into sleep, waiting for him to begin. He lay awake a long time thinking. He was sober and serious and he ached to pace and smoke; but he lay and held her in his arms, not moving, so that her sleep wasn't disturbed.

Ten

___

On Monday all the children at Sara's school were just like all the other kids after spring break. They were full of exuberance from their holiday, and it would take a while for them to settle down and pay attention.

Sara mentioned that to Mike with a fond sigh of impatience.

Then, in an office visit to have Dan change his patch, Mike heard the people in the waiting room talking.

He asked Dan about it.

"Sara's the instigator," Dan explained. "Ask her."

So that night, he did. "What have you to do with all the chatter around town about keeping the kids busy this last week?"

And she told him.

Since there were kids who didn't get to go away from Byford on spring break, Sara had garnered permission for the kids to use the school library and the gym. Those two sections had outside doors and could be isolated from the rest of the building.

Three other teachers had gone in with Sara to hire two retired teachers to monitor the kids for that week. And the four had rattled the bushes to find volunteers who would help those two, and more cripplingly impressive, they'd *scheduled* them!

The planning had begun last fall. They'd had to pay temporary insurance and wade through a lot of red tape.

"We rented one of those humongous TVs. And from the school library the kids could see the 'Discovery' tapes, those from the *National Geographic* and those from the 'Wild Wild World of Animals.'" It had been Sara who'd paid for the TV rental.

"So those at-home kids have also 'seen' faraway places." She cast a huge sigh. "The whole thing was a real hassle—we aren't sure we'll *ever* do it again!" But she grinned as she shook her head.

Mike's first reaction was that the instigators had been stupid. How like a bunch of teachers to organize kids on a vacation. Then, as he went around Byford on errands, he began to hear the parents' enthusiasm and especially the single mothers who'd been so grateful.

He mentioned that to Sara.

She said, "Herbert was present each day. You have to know that wasn't a surprise, but *Teddy* was enthusiastic."

Then the mayor said the other elementary schools in town ought to be included. Byford should take over the organization and seek the volunteers and pay for such a program. The Park Board had some resources and the means to help out. And George said the Jaycees could contribute. So Mike did, too.

It was a good idea. And it made Mike look at Sara more closely. He'd already thought she was a good woman, but she really thought about other people. She loved kids. And she did something about them.

He went over to see Rod, and sat and talked and beat around the bush until finally he said, "I don't know what to do about Sara."

Rod replied, "I'm no judge. You'll have to make up your own mind."

So Mike talked about her and told Rod what a wonderful woman she was and all about the spring-break school plan she'd concocted. He told nothing about their private encounters, or their lovemaking or anything like that, but he talked on and on and ON about Sara and how perfect she was. "I'm not good enough for her."

Rod listened. At first he was somewhat strained, because he didn't know how to advise Mike, but gradually he realized that Mike didn't need any response or advice, he simply wanted to talk about Sara.

Finally up to his ears in Sara's praise, Rod inquired, "You do know that you're in love with her?"

Mike shook his head in logical denial. "No." He was gentle in explaining. "I do admire her." He did admit that. "She is a prime example of womanhood, but I'm not zonked." And he put another piece of gum in his mouth to chew as he looked away, out the door. He didn't see anything. "I'll be in touch," he said to Rod.

It was that day, just before supper, that there was a knock on Sara's front door. Without any premonition, Mike went and opened it. A man stood there. Mike said, "Yeah?"

The man looked at Mike with some interest and asked, "Does Sara Benton still live here?"

And Mike asked right back, "Who wants to know?"

"I'm John Benton. Her dad."

An abandoned child himself, Mike reacted as if the man had been a rejecting part of his own life and he felt indignant. He was organizing his snide response, when Sara called, "Who is it?"

And not moving from his blocking stance in the doorway, Mike said, "He says he's your... father."

"Really?" Sara came from the kitchen into the living room, moving her head to see who was there.

Protectively Mike barely moved sideways, but only enough so that she could see the man.

She smiled a little. "Hello."

"Sara."

"Come inside," she invited, opening the door wider so that there was room to pass the blocking figure of her love. She smiled past Mike, at the man who called himself John Benton.

He returned her smile, but he looked then at Mike. "May I?"

"Got any ID?"

"Mi-iike," she chided.

"No, honey, he's right," John agreed. "Just a minute. What'll you accept? I have my Social Security card, my driver's license?"

"Those can be forged."

"Mike!"

"He's right, you know. Let's see—" John stayed on the porch and thought. "I think Bud Cameron down the block would identify me."

"He died last year." Sara watched her father.

"No. I'm sorry to hear that."

"How about Mrs. Morey?"

"Oh, she'd certainly remember me. She thought your mother was wrong to've ever married me. And she was right."

"Mother loved you."

"She was a sweet girl. You look like her, do you know that?"

Sara nodded. "People tell me that."

"I was traveling when she died. I was sorry not to be here for you."

"People were around." She looked up at Mike. "Do let him come inside—it's still quite cool."

Mike was thin-lipped and hostile. He was astounded she could carry on a conversation with this man and even courteously invite him into her house. He stepped back minimally.

John smiled up at Mike and said kindly, "I do understand."

Mike hardened his heart. It was some man just like this one who had fathered him and left him to drift out into the world alone. If it hadn't been for Salty and Felicia, he'd've had no home at all. He would have had no guidance. Anything could have happened to him. He'd been a throwaway child.

This man was just such a man. He had abandoned Sara, leaving her young mother alone to survive, with no help from him. Mike kept his stare on the man who claimed to be Sara's father. Mike's face was watchfully protective and rock-hard.

Sara was saying, "This is Mike Brown, who is staying here as my guest."

"Yeah," acknowledged John Benton. "I saw you on television. Byford loves a hero."

He was trying to ingratiate himself. Mike didn't respond at all. He narrowed his eyes at the bloodsucker.

Sara coaxed, "Sit down. Tell me about yourself. Can you stay for supper? There's enough."

"That would be fine."

And Mike's eyes were very hard. John Benton was moving in on his daughter. The bloodsucking bastard was broke and old, and he was probably looking for a soft cushion. He'd decided to return to his abandoned daughter.

"You've kept the house well." John glanced around. "It looks nice."

"It's been a godsend."

Awkwardly choosing his words, the returned deserter inquired, "How have you managed? I've thought about you so many times, wondering how you were getting along."

Mike almost burst a blood vessel. He shifted his feet and took a quick breath.

Sara glanced at Mike and invited, "Do sit down. Supper is just about ready."

She thought he was trying to be a host? He was her only defense against this intruder! Didn't she feel any uneasiness at all?

"Would you happen to have a beer?" John Benton inquired gently with a little smile.

And Mike felt hostile. The bloodsucker wanted some of *his* beer to—

Sara said, "We do! We just got some not long ago. Mike, would you get us each one?"

His beer! Mike glanced at his love and said, "Yeah." And he gave John Benton a very serious look as he strode across the room, hitting his heels against the carpet so that the basement sounded dull thuds back. He went into the kitchen and quickly uncapped three beers, pouring Sara's quietly into a glass. And he listened the entire time.

Sara was asking, "Are you staying for a while?"

John replied, "I haven't much time."

"Where are your things?"

"Down at the hotel on the square. I saw Melvin Piker. He recognized me. He was surprised I'd come around."

"I am, too, but it's wonderful to see you. Mother missed you so."

"Yes." The word was sad.

Mike thought: Damn him! Mike ground his teeth.

Mike sat through supper, eating in a rigid manner, contributing nothing but single words, as Sara tried to include him in the conversation. He was so hostile to Sara's father that he could not relax. It offended him that the man was eating Sara's food.

The man asked Sara, "How did you manage when you got your teaching degree?"

"When mother died, I was just finishing high school. Mr. Chambers at the bank, remember him? He said the bank would give me a second mortgage so that I could go to college over in Fort Wayne. It covered the car, so that I could drive over. I did manage.

But it was because of Mr. Chambers. We didn't have that much equity in the house."

"Bless him. Is he still around?"

"No. He died soon after I graduated. Do you know what he did? He came to my graduation. Wasn't that nice of him?"

John Benton wiped his eyes surreptitiously and cleared his throat.

The damned fraud. Mike was just glad he was there to protect Sara from this freeloading parasite.

Sara and John's conversation continued as they became acquainted. It would have been fascinating if Mike hadn't been so adamantly opposed to the man. He found something wrong or threatening about everything John Benton uttered. And Mike was ready to defend and protect Sara. It was a futile stance.

Sara was charmed by her father. Her conversation and questions and explanations were kind and curious as she obtained family information. Things remembered. Things about the Bentons that she'd never known.

John was sparse in his relating what had occurred to himself in the last thirty years.

Mike figured he'd been in jail.

And finally John told of his remarriage. "It was after I read that your mother had died. I'd become . . . involved with a lady. We married. She was not a strong woman. We could have no children. She died just recently.

"I'm sorry."

"Yes."

Mike said nothing.

Finally John Benton said, "It's getting late. I know you have to get up early to go to school—"

"Will you come tomorrow?"

John looked at Mike for permission.

Mike looked at Sara, giving it.

Sara said, "I would be so pleased to see you again. Would you like to stay here? Mike and I can share my room."

"No. Thank you, Sara. I'm comfortable down at the hotel. I can only stay a day or so longer."

"I'll take tomorrow off on personal leave. We can have the day together."

John replied, "That would be so nice."

Sara was pleased. "Then I'll do it." She walked with her father, looping her arm in his. She kissed his cheek. She looked outside. Then she looked up and down the street. "Where is your car?"

"I took a cab."

"I'll take you back downtown."

Mike said, "I'll drive."

So the two sat in the backseat, while Mike drove her father and Sara downtown. It wasn't far. It seemed to take a long time.

At the curb, Sara got out with her father and again kissed his cheek. He hugged her gently. Mike got out and went around the car to open the car door for Sara to sit in front.

A man came from the hotel and walked past them, speaking to Sara. He walked another several steps before he stopped and turned back. "Is it John Benton?"

And John replied, "Yes. Paul?"

And Paul laughed. "Good to see you!" He strode over and held out his hand. "Visiting?"

"For just a couple of days. I have go get back. I saw Sara on television with your celebration. I was traveling and took the opportunity to come and see her again."

"You got a good one in that girl."

Sara corrected snippily, "Woman."

And the two older men chuckled gently.

Paul then said, "If you have time, come by my office. I'm still upstairs over across the square."

"Not this time. Thanks, Paul." Then he turned to Sara and said, "I'll see you in the morning. Good night, daughter."

"Good night, Dad."

Sara stood watching until her father went from her sight.

Mike waited.

Sara turned and smiled at Mike. She got into the car and sighed happily. Mike carefully closed the door, went around and got into the driver's seat.

They drove almost all the way back to Sara's in silence. Sara wore a happy little smile and a dreamy expression. Mike was a cauldron of seething indignation.

He asked through his teeth, "How could you be that courteous to a man who left you and your mother that long ago? You never heard from him in all that time?"

"It's so interesting to see him! To hear what he has to say. You must remember that I've no memory of talking to him. I suppose at five I did have exchanges with him, but it wasn't about what he thought of things or what I thought of them.

"We have a picture of him. It was one taken the day they were married. They were so young. With the picture, you can see him in the man he is now."

"Not much."

"Have you seen the picture?"

"No. He's not much."

"Now, Michael, he's my father. You must be courteous."

"I resent him landing on you after all these years."

"I'm delighted he came. This is a gift! My curiosity has been so niggling. I've wondered if he was still alive. I figured I'd never again see him."

"You be careful."

"I was cheated out of thirty years of knowing him. I don't want to lose the rest of the time I can see him."

"He's a potential millstone."

"Aren't we all?"

"God, Sara, you're such a softy."

"About . . . several people."

"I want to be . . ." But he stopped himself.

"What do you want to be? I'll help."

And she would. He knew that. But he couldn't quite say the words.

So they went to bed in Sara's room that night and Mike used all the skill he'd acquired and dreamed of using in making love to her. She was so sweet and tender with him that she almost had another vulture standing around rattling his feathers, living off her.

When she slept, Mike eased from her bed and paced, chewing gum. Gradually he faced the problem, the reason he was so disturbed. It was Sara's father's arrival that was nagging at him. It reminded Mike and underlined the fact that his own parents had both vanished and left him alone in a desert of people. He belonged to no one.

That strong, hard Mike stood in the kitchen and looked out back on Sara's woodlot shadows. That was what the world had always looked like to Mike. A dense forest of people, none of whom he recognized. He was alone in the world. No kith nor kin. And he finally allowed the acknowledgment of the fact that he felt that way.

He'd always been aloof. He'd never allowed himself any close relationships, not because he was aloof, but because he wasn't one of them, one of the world. He'd been thrown away. Unwanted.

All his actions were triggered by self-preservation. He could survive without anyone else. He was strong. He'd had to prove that to himself.

And Mike finally understood himself.

Salty and Felicia had given him shelter and direction. They gave him affection and humor, too, but he'd not accepted that. He'd lost himself in the safety of their extended household of actual, adopted and harbored children. He was one of a group to which he belonged, but without attachment.

And he understood why the army had been perfect for him. Again, he was one of a cohesive group that had discipline and purpose. It was a place to be useful, to learn, to be with other people who were constantly shifted around but of a larger group to which he could belong, again without attachment.

He didn't know how to break off and go on his own. But there was Sara.

If ever he proposed to make a life beyond his work and those casual acquaintances, he must begin. Could he?

His longing for children had included no thought of having his own. He could raise children, those discarded by someone else. He could make another group. While he could rescue unwanted children and help them the way Salty and Felicia had, he didn't know how to share love well enough to nurture babies.

Sara did.

Could he learn?

And he wondered if his parents should ever show up on his doorstep, could he be as welcoming and uncritical as Sara had been? Could he accept them as of that minute? Or would he blame and rail because he had never known who he was?

Who was he?

So the next morning, as Sara stirred in his arms, he said, "I'm going to leave you and your dad alone today. I think I'll go over to see Rod."

"Oh," she said in disappointment. "I would like you to know him, too."

"Sara, you're a special lady. You scare me. I'm not sure I should even touch your hand."

She laughed. "Silly."

He leaned over her and looked at her very seriously. "You're a dream woman."

"I belch. Do I snore?"

"Bubbles."

"How rude of you!" She mussed his short hair. "Bring Rod home with you, if you like."

"You're wonderful."

"Not perfect?" She pulled on his ears to bring his face close, so that he had to kiss her. "You'll be home for supper?"

Something else had just occurred to Mike, and he replied, "If I'm . . . delayed, I'll call."

Sara turned thoughtful. She watched him for a minute and she was very still. She said, "Take care of yourself."

He smiled into her eyes, and he kissed her again.

Rod came to the shop early, as he always did, and found his brother Mike waiting for him. "She finally get smart and throw you out?"

But Mike was serious. "I've been thinking."

"That's always a mistake."

"We were very lucky to have Salty find us."

"Yes." Mike's tone and words had captured Rod's close attention and he watched his adoptive brother.

"I don't think I ever really understood that."

"Sometimes things take a while."

"I'm going over to thank them. Want to come along?"

Rod considered. Then he said, "This is something you need to do alone."

Mike moved his feet a couple of steps. "Yeah." He looked then at Rod and offered his hand. Rod took it with a firm, warm grasp.

Rod watched as Mike drove away. Then he debated almost an hour, before he called Salty and just said, "Mike's coming over. He's okay. He just wanted to see you again before he goes back to his base."

It took a good five hours of driving to get to Temple. Mike didn't even listen to the radio. He spent the time sorting out his thinking. All the feelings and problems and attitudes that he'd kept shoved down below his conscious channels.

It was with some irony that, at age thirty-six, he considered he might be maturing.

Mike got back to Temple at almost two that afternoon. The kids were still in school. As soon as he drew up, Salty and Felicia were out on the porch. They'd been looking for him?

"Hi, hero." As Salty hugged his adopted son, his words were raspy with pride. "CNN picked up some of the celebration in Byford. We taped it for the family archives."

See? They considered him "family," with history and events that were important to the Browns. Why hadn't he ever realized that before now?

Mike was hugging Felicia as he scoffed. "Getting hit by shrapnel isn't heroic. It's being in the wrong place."

"But you were there."

Felicia watched him; her big eyes narrowed just the slightest. And Mike realized it was Felicia who knew everything. If a child was troubled or someone felt ill, she always knew. Sara would, too.

Salty was the monitor of behavior, and Felicia watched for problems. What a team.

"I can't stay long," Mike explained. "I had to come back and just see you again."

They smiled, and Felicia's eyes became a bit moist. "Come inside," she invited in her marvelous throaty voice.

They went into the living room before a small fire in the fireplace. "Tea?" asked Felicia.

"Beer?" asked Salty.

"Coffee?" Mike inquired with a grin.

And Salty went to fetch some.

Felicia asked casually, "Who was that gorgeous woman in the blue dress?"

"That's Sara." Mike voice was earnest. "I'm thinking about her."

"Ahh." Felicia made the simple sound very telling.

Mike smiled. "Yeah. Just that way."

"Good."

Salty returned. "What have I missed?"

Felicia responded: "He's considering the lady in the blue dress."

"What's her name?"

"Sara Benton."

They both nodded as they exchanged a glance.

And Mike suddenly remembered the exquisite silent communication that had always passed between the two! How could he have been so unseeing?

"I need to talk before the kids get home. I came to tell you, Thank you. I'm only now appreciating all that you two did for me. You, this...home, all the family. I don't know words to tell you how important you are to me."

Felicia smiled and widened her eyes, trying to keep from leaking tears, so it was Salty who replied, "It was mutual. You've done well. You're a good man. You're only now realizing it."

"No. I'm only realizing how important you are to me," he repeated. "I was so caught by the fact that my parents had discarded me, that I couldn't think beyond that to another relationship. Only now do I understand, and it's because of Sara."

He then told about Sara's father coming to see her. He told of his reaction to that, then he explained Sara's, and how her response had affected him. How it had made him think of himself and of his own adoptive family.

"We knew you'd come to understand this sometime." Felicia was kind. "That you would know how much you are a part of us. But you must think of your parents with compassion. We were never able to trace them. But you weren't a 'throwaway' child. Whoever they were, they were unable to keep you. This was to our advantage. You are ours."

"I came to say, Thank you." He needed to say it again.

"You're welcome. You truly are, Michael. We love you."

Salty blew his nose. "This is one of those soggy times that are hard to plow through, but it's important that the words are said. You gotta understand how much you mean to us. You always have. And if you think you've had problems adjusting to the family, think of Cray. You were over in that war when he came home, but he'd had a tough time for almost four years, trying to get sorted out. And he was a kid we made."

And another facet of living was revealed to Mike. Kids who were the genetic offspring could be as unsettled and difficult as those adopted or harbored.

Mike shook his head over the struggle of living.

Salty said, "Don't ever forget that whatever happens, it almost always balances. It's all worthwhile."

"You two are unique."

They denied it.

When it came time to call Sara, Mike didn't know how to say the things he wanted to say to her, and he didn't make the call.

So Mike went back to Byford and arrived at Sara's house at eleven that night. She'd left a light on for him, so she'd expected him to return. He'd been shown the spare house key's hiding place, so he felt that he could go inside.

Dressed in nightclothes, wearing that pink lacy wrapper, she came from her room, her face was serious. "Are you all right?"

He looked at a dream woman. The most beautiful woman in all the world, and he knew. He said, "I've been home. I went to see Felicia and Salty who are my adoptive parents."

"Salty? The cook?"

"He was a navy man. He adopted three of us before he married Felicia. Sara, I really was an orphan. I allowed you to believe I had no place to go so that you'd allow me to get a toehold in here."

"Ahh." She considered him. "Rod and Cray?"

"Yeah. There are others."

"In the 'home?' "

"Altogether, Salty and Felicia have cared for or adopted about twenty-three kids. They had five of their own. We'll go over there next weekend, and you can meet Salty and Felicia and some of the kids."

"Yes." She seemed distracted. "Twenty-*eight?*"

"Give or take a few. When you were with your dad, I went over there to thank them for adopting me. You taught me that appreciation when you welcomed your dad so kindly. I learned a lot from you."

"Oh, Mike—"

"I want to marry you."

She gasped. Then she smiled a little. And then she laughed. "What a proposal! For Pete's sake, Michael! You have to do better than that!"

Very seriously, he went down on his knees and held out his arms. "I love you, Sara. Are you brave enough to marry me?"

She considered him seriously as she went to him and knelt before him. She replied, "For the rest of your life and wherever you go, I would like to be with you. Yes."

Mike smiled and tears clung to his lower lashes. But he had to be honest with her. "You have to know I'm not a hero. It was the war that made it seem as if I'm different. I'm not. I'm just a man."

"You are a hero. But it wasn't the war that made you one, it was you."

Their kiss was so gentle as they knelt facing one another. His arms held her gently and his hands cherished her. He stood up and lifted her into his arms. He stood there in the softness of her beacon light left to guide him home, and he looked at his precious woman. "My God, Sara, I do love you."

"I thought so, but I'm glad you admit it."

"What made you think so?"

"When you gutted my car, so that I couldn't throw you out of my house."

"Dead giveaway?"

She shook her head. "Not even subtle."

"You didn't object."

"I'd been in love with you for months."

"The picture in your purse?"

"Now, how did you know about that?"

"I locked my keys in the car, and you were in the bathr—"

"And you didn't even *mention* it!"

"No." He smiled just a tiny, tiny bit.

"So you were sure of me."

"Yeah."

"Why didn't you tell me?" she scolded.

"You already knew."

"I only suspected."

"Will you live with me in that bare little apartment down in Texas and make it into a paradise?"

"You want feather fans and grapes dropped into your mouth?"

"Let's try that."

She laughed, and he carried her to her room. They stripped and climbed onto the bed where they made wondrous love. Again it was different, profound, amazing. They sighed and murmured and touched and smoothed. They rubbed and squeezed and wiggled and writhed. And they made sounds and gasped. They resisted as long as possible before they were whirled into the rapturous spiral to ride the tumultuous winds of passionate ecstasy to reach paradise.

And it was there for them.

Some time later Mike asked his lady, who was floating in a misty haze, "Are we going to have some babies?"

"How soon?"

"Well, self-produced, they take a while."

She admitted, "I'd heard that."

"We could get a head start," he suggested.

"Oh?" she inquired cautiously.

"We could adopt a couple."

A little more open, she replied, "That might be nice."

"Sometimes it takes a while to get them to fit in." He offered that newly acquired knowledge.

She regarded her love.

He planned: "We'll be like the cops. You know— good cop, bad cop? I'll be the Good Dad, and you can be the Bad Mo—"

"Uhh. Hold it!"

And he settled down contentedly to share and debate and listen and argue. He was half of a couple.

* * * * * *

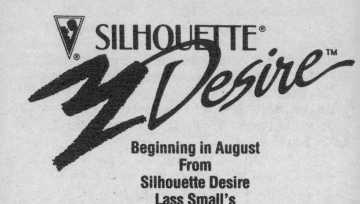

SILHOUETTE® *Desire*™

**Beginning in August
From
Silhouette Desire
Lass Small's
Fabulous Brown Brothers**

When the Brown Brothers are good, they're very, very good.
But when they're bad . . . they are fabulous!

Read about Creighton, Mike and Rod in Lass Small's upcoming
Fabulous Brown Brothers series. And see if you don't agree.

**In August—A RESTLESS MAN (SD #731)
In October—TWO HALVES (SD #743)
In December—BEWARE OF WIDOWS (SD #755)**

Boys will be boys . . . and these men are no exception!

It's Opening Night in October—
and you're invited!
Take a look at romance with a
brand-new twist, as the stars
of tomorrow make their
debut today!
It's LOVE:
an age-old story—
now, with
*WORLD PREMIERE
APPEARANCES* by:

Patricia Thayer—Silhouette Romance #895
JUST MAGGIE—Meet the Texas rancher who wins this pretty
teacher's heart...and lose your own heart, too!

Anne Marie Winston—Silhouette Desire #742
BEST KEPT SECRETS—Join old lovers reunited and see what
secret wonders have been hiding...beneath the flames!

Sierra Rydell—Silhouette Special Edition #772
ON MIDDLE GROUND—Drift toward Twilight, Alaska, with this
widowed mother and collide—heart first—into body heat
enough to melt the frozen tundra!

Kate Carlton—Silhouette Intimate Moments #454
KIDNAPPED!—Dare to look on as a timid wallflower blos-
soms and falls in fearless love—with her gruff, mysterious
kidnapper!

**Don't miss the classics of tomorrow—
premiering today—only from**

PREM

TAKE A WALK ON THE DARK SIDE OF LOVE

October is the shivery season, when chill winds blow and shadows walk the night. Come along with us into a haunting world where love and danger go hand in hand, where passions will thrill you and dangers will chill you. Come with us to

In this newest short story collection from Sihouette Books, three of your favorite authors tell tales just perfect for a spooky autumn night. Let Anne Stuart introduce you to "The Monster in the Closet," Helen R. Myers bewitch you with "Seawitch," and Heather Graham Pozzessere entice you with "Wilde Imaginings."

Silhouette Shadows™
Haunting a store near you this October.

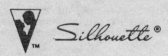